JOINED BY LOVE

Lucilla looked desperately towards Ethel, wishing that she might say something to make Harkness Jackson leave her alone.

But Ethel just smiled and then nodded her elegant blonde head, as if she had been planning this meeting all along.

"Come along, Mortimer dear," she cooed. "I don't think we are very welcome here just at the moment."

"Aha!" he exclaimed, gazing at his friend Harkness, still on his knees in front of Lucilla. "Sure, honey, let's go."

And the two of them left Lucilla alone in the salon, her hand caught in the big American's grasp.

"Please, will you let me go?" Lucilla begged him, struggling to keep her voice steady.

"Lady Lucilla," Harkness began, clutching her hand even tighter. "Princess! I was all set to call on you this afternoon – but you have come to me instead!"

"I – didn't know that you would be here," Lucilla managed to say, "I came to visit Ethel – "

Harkness was not listening.

"From the first moment I set eyes on you," he was saying, "I knew you were the girl for me. I've waited a long time to find a wife and now I've found her. I ain't gonna to beat about the bush. What do you say, Lucilla? Will you be mine? "

THE BARBARA CARTLAND PINK COLLECTION

Titles in this series

JOINED BY LOVE

BARBARA CARTLAND

Barbaracartland.com Ltd

Printed and bound in Great Britain
by Mimeo of Huntingdon, Cambridgeshire.

THE BARBARA CARTLAND PINK COLLECTION

Dame Barbara Cartland is still regarded as the most prolific bestselling author in the history of the world.

In her lifetime she was frequently in the Guinness Book of Records for writing more books than any other living author.

Her most amazing literary feat was to double her output from 10 books a year to over 20 books a year when she was 77 to meet the huge demand.

She went on writing continuously at this rate for 20 years and wrote her very last book at the age of 97, thus completing an incredible 400 books between the ages of 77 and 97.

Her publishers finally could not keep up with this phenomenal output, so at her death in 2000 she left behind an amazing 160 unpublished manuscripts, something that no other author has ever achieved.

Barbara's son, Ian McCorquodale, together with his daughter Iona, felt that it was their sacred duty to publish all these titles for Barbara's millions of admirers all over the world who so love her wonderful romances.

So in 2004 they started publishing the 160 brand new Barbara Cartlands as *The Barbara Cartland Pink Collection*, as Barbara's favourite colour was always pink – and yet more pink!

The Barbara Cartland Pink Collection is published monthly exclusively by Barbaracartland.com and the books are numbered in sequence from 1 to 160.

Enjoy receiving a brand new Barbara Cartland book each month by taking out an annual subscription to the Pink Collection, or purchase the books individually.

The Pink Collection is available from the Barbara Cartland website www.barbaracartland.com via mail order and through all good bookshops.

In addition Ian and Iona are proud to announce that The Barbara Cartland Pink Collection is now available in ebook format as from Valentine's Day 2011.

For more information, please contact us at:

Barbaracartland.com Ltd.
Camfield Place
Hatfield
Hertfordshire AL9 6JE
United Kingdom

Telephone: +44 (0)1707 642629
Fax: +44 (0)1707 663041
Email: info@barbaracartland.com

THE LATE DAME BARBARA CARTLAND

Barbara Cartland who sadly died in May 2000 at the age of nearly 99 was the world's most famous romantic novelist who wrote 723 books in her lifetime with worldwide sales of over 1 billion copies and her books were translated into 36 different languages.

As well as romantic novels, she wrote historical biographies, 6 autobiographies, theatrical plays, books of advice on life, love, vitamins and cookery. She also found time to be a political speaker and television and radio personality.

She wrote her first book at the age of 21 and this was called *Jigsaw*. It became an immediate bestseller and sold 100,000 copies in hardback and was translated into 6 different languages. She wrote continuously throughout her life, writing bestsellers for an astonishing 76 years. Her books have always been immensely popular in the United States, where in 1976 her current books were at numbers 1 & 2 in the B. Dalton bestsellers list, a feat never achieved before or since by any author.

Barbara Cartland became a legend in her own lifetime and will be best remembered for her wonderful romantic novels, so loved by her millions of readers throughout the world.

Her books will always be treasured for their moral message, her pure and innocent heroines, her good looking and dashing heroes and above all her belief that the power of love is more important than anything else in everyone's life.

"Grey is a dull, lifeless and mediocre colour and it can hide unattractive and demeaning emotions. For me the glorious colour pink means the joy of life, the deep spiritual love between a man and a woman, the gentleness and intensity of a first kiss. Above all pink is the colour of love since time began and it will always be the same."

Barbara Cartland

CHAPTER ONE
1911

Lady Lucilla Welton stood by the French window of the magnificent ballroom at Lord Armstrong's mansion in Belgravia and hoped that no one would notice her.

The ballroom itself was packed with the rich and famous from London Society and the long mirrors on the walls reflected the brightly coloured gowns of the ladies and the elegant evening dress of the gentlemen.

It was the engagement party given for Ethel, Lord Armstrong's eldest daughter and Lucilla realised that there were some important guests amongst the gentlemen and many were Members of Parliament and influential figures from the worlds of industry and finance.

Her pale-blue satin gown, bought especially for the occasion, was in the very latest French style and it clung to her slim body in graceful folds, while a tight belt of velvet ribbon accentuated her slender waist.

This gown was the loveliest she had ever worn and Lucilla could tell from the glimpses she caught of herself in the mirrors that the colour showed off her shining brown hair and her huge blue eyes to perfection.

But Lucilla did not know anyone at the party and she felt shy under the curious glances of the dark-suited men who were milling around the edges of the ballroom.

1

Some of these men, she knew, were from America, and were friends and associates of Ethel's fiancé, who was a wealthy financier from New York.

'I should feel flattered that these gentlemen are looking at me,' Lucilla thought, 'but I don't know any of them. I am just a country girl at heart and so I really don't feel comfortable here at all.'

She watched the elegant Society ladies laughing and chatting away with the gentlemen and then standing up to dance with them, and she thought that they did not seem embarrassed in the slightest.

Lucilla sighed and wished that she could escape to her home in the beautiful Dorset countryside, but this was impossible.

For the last year she had been living with her Aunt Maud, since both her parents had been killed in a dreadful and tragic accident while they were on holiday in the Swiss Alps.

Aunt Maud had taken her orphaned niece into her London home and was making every effort to transform her into a London Society girl – even buying the heavenly pale-blue gown for her – and Lucilla knew that she should be grateful.

It was just very hard to be happy, when she missed her Mama and Papa so very much, and simply longed to be back home again at their lovely country house, Wellsprings Place, which – she could hardly bear to think of it – was now up for sale.

"Oh, I so wish I was back in Dorset," she groaned. "By the sea, breathing in the fresh air, listening to the birds singing – "

She blushed, as she realised she had been speaking out loud and that a stout gentleman with a head so totally bald that it shone under the light of the glittering crystal chandelier, had seen her talking to herself and was smiling at her.

"Lucilla, darling!"

A tall girl in a white and silver dress was coming towards her, clicking across the floor in her pointed silver shoes.

It was Ethel, the bride-to-be.

Lucilla admired the shimmering dress, the skirt of which was so fashionably tight and narrow that Ethel could only take very small steps as she walked towards her.

She was very attractive, Lucilla thought, with her white-blonde hair and her pale green eyes, but at the same time, there was something cool, almost icy, about her.

"I must find a partner for you," Ethel was saying, and she took Lucilla's hand in her cool slim one and tried to lead her away from the window.

"No, really, I am quite happy just here," Lucilla replied and she tried to explain that she did not really know anyone at the party and was feeling rather shy and a bit tired.

But there was no resisting Ethel.

"Don't be ridiculous," she said, tucking Lucilla's hand under her arm. "If you don't know anyone, that's all the more reason to get up and dance. You'll never meet anybody if you behave like a wallflower."

"Oh, all right," Lucilla agreed, following Ethel, as she could see that the bald-headed man was looking at her again and she did not want to have to speak to him.

On the other side of the ballroom, a tall young man with dark hair was sitting on a sofa reading a book and Ethel led Lucilla over to him.

"Dermot, I have just found you the most delicious partner," she called out to him, pushing Lucilla forward.

"Isn't she just the prettiest thing? And totally unspoilt – just perfect for you!"

Lucilla was surprised to hear a note of bitterness in Ethel's voice and she winced as she grasped her wrist, holding it so tightly that her nails dug in.

The dark-haired young man looked up from his book and stared at Ethel, his brown eyes devouring her face hungrily.

"What are you trying to do, Ethel?" he countered in a low voice. "If you don't want me, then why cannot you just leave me alone?"

Ethel's pale eyes turned bright, as if she was trying not to cry.

"Don't be silly, Dermot. I just want to make you feel better, that's all."

"Well, you can't!" he asserted and, turning away from them, began reading his book again.

Ethel then shrugged angrily and hurried off, leaving Lucilla standing awkwardly by the sofa.

She watched Ethel wipe the back of her slim hand across her eyes and then turn with a bright smile, as her fiancé, a tall distinguished man with grey hair, came up to her.

"It's Mortimer van Millingen," Lucilla whispered, watching the man's grey head stooping to kiss Ethel's hand. "He's a stockbroker, isn't he? From New York?"

"I neither know nor care," the young man retorted sharply. "And, if you are looking for a dancing partner, I suggest that you try elsewhere, as I have no intention of prancing around with anyone this evening."

Lucilla jumped, startled by his rudeness.

"I am so sorry," she mumbled. "I interrupted your reading. I didn't mean – "

The young man looked up at her with a frown and then away again quickly and Lucilla felt a pang in her heart as she could see a look of pain in his brown eyes.

Perhaps he was being so rude and abrupt because he was upset about something, she thought to herself.

"Excuse me, sir," she said, "I will not trouble you any further."

And she slipped away from his side and made her way over the crowded ballroom towards a white-and-gold painted door, which she hoped might lead somewhere more private.

As she dodged the dancing couples, she noticed the bald-headed man again talking to Mortimer van Millingen and peering around as if he was looking for someone.

'I do hope he isn't looking for me!' she thought and then sighed with relief as she opened the door and slipped through, finding herself in a small salon, furnished with several gilt chairs and a shining grand piano.

She closed the door behind her and the hubbub of music and chatter from the ballroom sank to a whisper.

Lucilla went over to the piano and sat down on the velvet stool.

She lifted the polished gleaming lid and touched the ivory keys.

Since she was a child, Lucilla had loved music and her Mama, who was a brilliant pianist, had taught her to play extremely well.

One of the factors that made Lucilla saddest about coming to live with her aunt was that there was no piano in her tall redbrick house in Maida Vale.

'I'll just play one piece,' she decided and found her fingers picking out the tender notes of a Chopin *étude* – one of her Papa's favourites.

In an instant, she was lost in the magical world of the music and it was almost as if she was back in the music room at Wellsprings Place, with the wind rustling in the trees outside and her dear Papa sitting by the fire, his foot softly tapping in time to her notes.

The door to the salon opened and Lucilla looked up with a start to see that the bald-headed man had come in and was leaning against the door so that no one else could enter.

He smiled at her and waved his hand, indicating for her to keep on playing.

"Please don't stop on my behalf," he called out in a strong American accent. "That tune – it's real cute."

Lucilla's fingers slipped on the keys and hit two wrong notes at once.

"I'm sorry," she sighed, getting up from the piano stool, "but I really should go back to the ball."

Her heart skipped a beat, as she realised that she could not leave the salon without pushing past this man and he showed no sign of moving, but carried on leaning against the door.

"Shall we dance, then?" he suggested with a laugh, dodging from side to side and blocking Lucilla's way as she tried to edge past him.

"Seriously, honey, I've been tryin' to figure out a way to get you for my partner all evening. You must be the cutest little thing in the ballroom."

Lucilla felt her cheeks grow fiery hot, for he was staring at her with his little grey eyes in a way that made her feel most uncomfortable.

"Hellooo!"

There was a commotion outside the door and Lady Armstrong's head appeared as she pushed it open.

"Oh! There you are, Harkness! I didn't realise you were a connoisseur of music."

"Oh yes, ma'am!" the man grinned. "Can't resist, especially when there's a pretty gal playin'."

"Harkness! You are really a naughty old so-and-so," Lady Armstrong smiled.

"This lovely creature is Lady Lucilla Welton. From Dorset. Terrible tragedy," she went on in a lower voice. "Both parents lost, very sad."

Lucilla looked through the open door behind Lady Armstrong and longed to escape, but her Ladyship was still there talking now in a much louder voice.

"Lucilla, dear, this is Mr. Harkness Jackson from America. A friend of my future-son-in-law, Mortimer. Mr. Harkness owns quite a number of oil wells, I believe!"

And then Lady Armstrong fluttered her eyelashes at the American.

Someone else had now come to the door and was looking into the salon.

"I thought I heard someone playing Chopin?"

It was the young man with the dark hair, who had been sitting reading a book on the sofa.

"Yes – it was me." Lucilla piped up.

She wanted to speak to him, as she thought he was still looking rather sad, but Harkness Jackson had caught hold of her hand.

"Lady Lucilla, I claim the next dance," he grinned. "And let anyone who tries to cut in look out for himself!"

Lucilla shivered at the touch of his thick hands on her arm and on her waist, and tried to hold herself away from him as he spun her around on the dance floor, but it was rather difficult, as he was quite overweight and kept pulling her against his bulky waistcoat.

She knew that Harkness Jackson's grey eyes were staring down at her, but she could not look up at him.

Instead, she looked out for the young man with the dark hair and the sad brown eyes, but the sofa where he had been sitting was empty and he was nowhere to be seen amongst the other dancers.

"One more dance, honey!" Harkness insisted, as the waltz began to draw to a close.

"I am feeling rather tired," Lucilla said, trying to pull her hand from his.

"You English girls!" he laughed and he raised her hand to his lips and kissed it. "Off you go then, run away from me! But I'll catch up with you again soon, little Lady Lucilla!"

Lucilla's legs were trembling as she made her way to the entrance hall of Lady Armstrong's mansion.

"My wrap, please," she said to the butler, who was standing by the front door. "And – would you see if my carriage has arrived yet? I have an awful headache and I should like to go right away."

She knew that it was very rude of her to leave early, but she just could not face another dance with Harkness Jackson.

The butler brought her velvet wrap and helped her to drape it around her shoulders.

"Your carriage arrived a few minutes ago and is waiting for you on the drive, my Lady. I shall inform her Ladyship that you are unwell and have gone home."

Lucilla made her way down the front steps to the carriage and felt the cool air blowing across her forehead.

'How lovely,' she told herself. 'I have escaped and I need never see that man ever again!'

And there was a smile on her lips as she lay back on the cushions and felt the wheels of the carriage bumping over the cobblestones.

*

Next morning, a robin was singing outside Lucilla's bedroom window and the sweet notes broke into her sleep.

For an instant she felt she was in her bedroom at Wellsprings Place and she could almost smell the delicious crisp bacon, the fresh-baked bread and the fragrant coffee that was always served at breakfast in her old home.

But when she opened her eyes, instead of her own pretty white furniture and rose-patterned curtains, she saw the dark wooden wardrobe and the drab green walls of the small bedroom her aunt had allocated to her.

On the other side of the net-curtained window, the robin sang bravely on, perched high in the bare branches of a plane tree in the street outside.

'How can that little bird keep singing in the middle of London and in February, when everything is so dismal and grey?' Lucilla thought.

And as she dressed and went down to breakfast, she decided to follow the robin's example and be as cheerful and bright as she could.

Her Aunt Maud was already seated at the table and gave Lucilla a black look as she came in, for she insisted on punctuality at mealtimes.

"If I have seen fit, out of the kindness of my heart, to offer you board and lodging, the least you can do is turn up in good time for the food that is prepared for you," she grumbled, as she had done on so many previous occasions.

Lucilla smiled at her aunt and apologised politely, although her heart sank at the sight of the vast tureen of porridge in the middle of the table.

If only, just once, they could have some delicious fried bacon!

"I hope you slept well, Aunt Maud," Lucilla said, as she spooned the thick porridge into her bowl.

"As a matter of fact," her aunt replied, looking at Lucilla down her long nose, "I did not. I had just retired to my bedroom, when I heard the carriage and I realised that you had returned from Lady Armstrong's. What were you thinking of, to leave so early?"

"I – had – a headache," Lucilla stammered.

Aunt Maud snorted with disapproval.

"And no wonder! If you ate the wholesome food that I provide for you, instead of finicking about with it, you would not be plagued with these ridiculous ailments."

Lucilla dipped her spoon in the grey porridge and tried to eat a mouthful of it, but it was tasteless and lumpy and made her feel sick.

"So, before your 'headache' overtook you, I trust that you made the most of all the Social opportunities that came your way?" Aunt Maud continued, a questioning look in her little green eyes. "To whom did you speak? And who asked you to dance?"

"I spoke to Ethel and I thought she looked very beautiful."

Aunt Maud shook her head.

"You are being absurdly irritating, Lucilla. Which *gentlemen* did you speak to?"

"Oh, there was a young man with dark hair – " Lucilla began.

"What was his name? Did you dance with him?"

"I didn't ask his name – and we didn't dance – "

Aunt Maud's long face was now turning red with annoyance.

"Do you know how much that pale-blue dress cost, young lady? I wanted you to look your very best, as Lady Armstrong told me that some of the wealthiest and most significant men in England – many of them still unmarried – would attend that party. Did you hide in the cloakroom all evening? Did you manage to dance with anyone at all?"

Lucilla felt a sharp chill run down her spine, as she thought of Mr. Harkness Jackson's heavy hand holding her waist.

"I did dance with an American gentleman, Aunt."

Aunt Maud sniffed.

"Some young bounder, no doubt."

"Oh, no. He is quite old and Lady Armstrong told me that he owned a lot of oil wells."

"Really?"

Aunt Maud's neck lengthened and Lucilla thought she looked like a hen, which has spied a tasty morsel of grain.

"Well, of course young Ethel has done so well for herself with her New York banker. The Armstrongs will never go short once she has tied the knot with him."

She smiled at Lucilla.

"You are very lucky you have your title, my dear, and a modicum of good looks, for you have very little else to recommend you. What was this gentleman's name?"

"Mr. Harkness – Jackson," Lucilla muttered and felt her throat catching on the words.

As she thanked her aunt for the porridge and asked if she might leave the table, Lucilla fervently hoped that she would never have to see that stout bald gentleman ever again.

*

The Marquis of Castlebury lay stretched out on the sofa in the drawing room at Appleton Hall, his ancestral home in Hampshire.

His head was propped on a round pillow which had a posy of white daisies embroidered on it.

"How could she do it to me, Violet?" he asked his elder sister, who was sitting opposite him on the other side of the fireplace and stitching some snowdrops onto a piece of cloth.

At her feet, a little black-and-white dog was curled up asleep in its basket, its pointed nose resting on its long legs.

"Dermot, I did tell you that you shouldn't go to the engagement party," Violet said, looking at her brother over gold-rimmed glasses. "I knew you would be upset."

"I had to go, Violet! I thought maybe she might see me and – change her mind."

The Marquis groaned and then buried his face in the pillow.

"Dermot, darling boy, please try and forget her. I am sure Ethel really does like you very much indeed, but the Armstrongs have been in financial trouble for a long time. And this American – "

"Mortimer! Mortimer van Millingen!" the Marquis hissed. "What a ridiculous name!"

"Ridiculous or not, he is supposed to be incredibly wealthy. And we are – well – we have enough money to be comfortable, but even with the income from the estate here at Castlebury, we would never have had enough to save Ethel and her family."

Violet's large brown eyes stung with tears as she looked at her brother's long limbs stretched out on the sofa with his dark curly head buried in a cushion.

She hated to see him unhappy.

It was still a shock to her, sometimes, to realise that he was a man now and the Head of the Family and not the cheerful little boy she had always loved and protected.

"It must have been just horrid for you," she sighed. "Was there anything nice at all about the party?"

The Marquis sat up and swung his long legs to the floor.

"Violet, I love you!" he cried. "You never fail to look for the good in everyone and everything."

He ran his hands through his curly hair, his eyes showing a spark of enthusiasm, as he continued,

"Actually, there were a good number of politicians there and I was telling some of them about the restoration work we've been doing here at Appleton. One of the MPs, a chap with some sort of responsibility for trade and export was bemoaning the fact that we have all these wonderful country houses and such glorious treasures here in England and nobody from abroad ever comes to see them."

"That's very true," Violet agreed. "I always come back to England after a trip away and think it's absolutely the most beautiful country in the world. And yet hardly any Europeans come to visit us, whereas we are always travelling to France, Italy and Germany."

"There is so much history tied up here and so many wonderful old buildings. So, this MP chap was asking me if I'd like to be an Ambassador, sort of, and go round some of the Cities in Europe to talk to people and persuade them to come over here and see some of our unique heritage."

"Yes!" Violet cried, laying her embroidery down and clasping her hands in excitement. "That's a wonderful idea! After all, the Americans really appreciate our history and they are coming over in droves."

The Marquis looked as if he might be about to subside into the pillow again and Violet realised she had said the wrong thing.

"Oh – Dermot, I didn't mean – "

"Yes, they are coming here and they're stealing our best girls as well!"

"You're just feeling bitter about Ethel."

"I am," the Marquis nodded ruefully. "I just cannot believe what she's done to me, Violet. She told me she loved me. And then she turned around and got engaged to this American, who's old enough to be her father by the look of him."

Violet did not like the gloomy depressed expression that was clouding her brother's handsome face.

She had never known him to be so unhappy before.

"I think it would be wonderful idea for you to go to Europe," she said. "It will be a change of scenery for you and you will meet all sorts of interesting people."

The Marquis sighed.

"I know what you are trying to do! You think, if I go off to Paris or somewhere and go to lots of receptions and parties, I'll meet another girl and fall in love. Well – I won't!"

Violet tried to encourage her brother, but he was not having any of it.

"I love Ethel and I know I'll never meet a woman who could take her place in my heart," he added bitterly.

He stood up and walked to the window to look out over the wintry park, where a soft rain was now falling over the trees.

"No, of course not. There will only ever be one Ethel," Violet agreed, thinking perhaps it would be wise to go along with him. "But Dermot – just think! Paris in the springtime – "

Her brother spun round, turning his back on the grey skies and the rain.

"All right, Violet. Maybe you have a point. I'll go and do this Ambassador thing, but only if you come with me!"

Violet tried not to show how much the thought of going abroad horrified her.

She loved her home at Appleton Hall so very much, especially the beautiful gardens, where she had planted so many rare and delicate specimens.

The thought of being away from the garden when the first bulbs would be coming out and leaving behind her precious little dog, Daisy, was most upsetting to her.

But more than anything else she loved her brother.

Violet then forced a bright smile onto her lips and enthused,

"Oh, Dermot! What a wonderful idea. I can't think of anything nicer. When shall we leave?"

As soon as Violet spoke these words, she knew she had made the right decision, as her brother's eyes were suddenly shining.

"Just as soon as we can, Violet! We are going to have *a great adventure*, I just know it!"

He strode from the window to hug his sister in his strong arms, as she valiantly hid the dread that welled up inside her, for a great adventure was the last thing Violet desired.

CHAPTER TWO

It was a grey and rainy morning several days after Ethel's engagement party, and Lucilla felt very despondent as she flicked a feather duster over the china ornaments on the corner cupboard in Aunt Maud's drawing room.

The fact that she was wearing an old cotton dress, and on top of it a big blue apron wrapped around to protect her from the dust did not help to raise her spirits.

Aunt Maud was sitting in her usual armchair by the fireplace, wearing blue fingerless mittens to keep her hands warm as she worked away at her crochet.

There was a fire in the grate, but it was a very small one, since Aunt Maud did not like to waste valuable coal, and the few flickering flames did not give off much heat.

"Oh, do be careful!" Aunt Maud scolded, frowning at Lucilla. "I don't like the way you are waving that duster so wildly. My china is priceless."

Lucilla apologised and then tried to be gentler, but it was difficult to reach the tallest of the ornaments without standing on tiptoe and holding the feather duster at arm's length and this made her aunt even more annoyed.

"Desist, you ridiculous girl!" she snorted, "you will have the whole lot on the floor in another moment. I shall have to find some other useful employment for you."

Lucilla stood on the rug in front of the fireplace and waited for her aunt to think of another tedious task for her to perform.

'If only there was a piano I could play,' she mused, as she had done every day since she had come to live with her aunt.

Even if she could only practice her scales, she knew that the sound of the notes would make her feel so much better and, surely, Aunt Maud would consider scales to be a suitable improving occupation for a young lady.

Suddenly, Lucilla heard a rusty squeak from the garden, which she knew meant that someone had opened the front gate.

"Aunt Maud, I think we have a visitor!" she said, forgetting herself and running to look out of the window.

Two elegant ladies were now walking slowly up the path, their fashionable narrow skirts causing them to take very small steps.

"I am not expecting anyone," Aunt Maud remarked with a frown. "But now you have forgotten all decorum and gone rushing to peer our through the curtains like some tradesman's wife, you might as well tell me who it is."

The two ladies were wearing stylish hats that were swathed in satin ribbons with veils of spotted net that hung down over their faces.

Lucilla detected a glint of white-blonde hair under the veil of the tallest lady.

"I think it might be Ethel and her Mama, Lady Armstrong!" she exclaimed.

Aunt Maud now stood up and pulled the fingerless mittens from her hands.

"Out of the way at once, Lucilla!" she ordered her. "Go to your room. And don't come down again until you have put on one of the new dresses I have bought for you. You look a perfect disgrace."

As Lucilla ran up the stairs, she heard a polite rat-a-tat at the front door and then her aunt's voice calling for the parlour maid, telling her not to answer the door until she had brought more coal for the fire.

When Lucilla came down the stairs again in a blue-and-white striped day dress that her aunt had given her to wear on special occasions, she heard voices coming from the drawing room.

She paused on the bottom step and held her breath to try and hear who was speaking.

"I really must apologise, Lady Armstrong, for the rudeness of my niece in leaving Ethel's party so early. I am doing my best with her – but really, she is still such a little country bumpkin!"

It was her Aunt Maud and Lucilla winced as she heard herself spoken about in such a disapproving way.

Next Lady Armstrong said something, but her voice was so quiet it was impossible to make out her words.

Aunt Maud began again,

"I have taken her in out of the kindness of my heart – and spared no expense to ensure that she has everything she needs. But it really is the most frightful inconvenience to be burdened with her at the moment."

Lucilla felt cold with misery as she heard this, but she could not stop listening.

She crept closer to the drawing room door.

Now she could hear Lady Armstrong more clearly.

"Ah – dear Mrs. Lewis. There is no doubt that you are the most generous of women. And at least Lucilla is a pretty little thing – "

Aunt Maud gave a snort.

"Indeed she is, your Ladyship. But to have a pretty girl always in the house is not ideal. As you know, Major

Lewis, my dear husband – so sadly missed – passed away almost five years ago now. The loss has been unendurable. And, now, when I find myself ready to – marry again – "

Lucilla heard aunt give a sniff, as if she was about to cry.

"My dear Mrs. Lewis!" Lady Armstrong's voice was warm and soft. "I quite understand. You have been alone too long. And – you are still a young woman."

"Oh, your Ladyship! You are indeed so wise and so insightful!" Aunt Maud sighed. "I am ready to embark upon the married state once more and I must confess there is a gentleman who is interested. But it is impossible with my niece in the house."

"Why?" Lucilla heard Ethel say. "Whatever do you mean?"

"Hush, dear," Lady Armstrong said to her daughter. "Of course Mrs. Lewis will not want to have a young and pretty girl at her dinner table when her beau comes round courting! That would not be appropriate or sensible – Mrs. Lewis will want his eyes to be on her alone!"

"You understand me perfectly, Lady Armstrong," said Aunt Maud. "It simply would not do. I wish to be married again and I will not have anything or anyone stand in my way. There must be no distractions or impediments to come between myself and the object of my affections."

There was a peal of laughter and then Lucilla heard Ethel's voice.

"Oh, Mama! Poor dear Lucilla! We must find a husband for *her* as quickly as we can and then everyone will be happy! But where is she?"

"I am here!" Lucilla exclaimed, stepping through the door. "I have just come down. I am so sorry to keep you waiting, Lady Armstrong."

"Why, my dear! Such a pretty dress. Those ruffles on the sleeves are just perfection," Lady Armstrong said, raising a gold eyeglass so she could peer at Lucilla through it.

"Thank you, ma'am," Lucilla sighed and gave a polite curtsy.

She tried to put out of her mind the conversation she had just overheard.

The fire was now blazing merrily and there was a tray of tea laid out beside it.

Ethel then rose to her feet and came over to Lucilla, kissing her on both cheeks as if they were best friends.

Lucilla was quite surprised by this, for she had only met Ethel once before, at the engagement party, and she was not at all sure that Ethel was someone she would like to have for a friend, as she seemed quite loud and rather overbearing.

"I'm so glad you were able to come to my party," Ethel was now saying, and then she whispered so that only Lucilla could hear, "you made quite an impression on a certain gentleman!"

Lucilla thought of the dark-haired young man, who had refused to dance with her.

She remembered the look in his brown eyes when he had come to the salon and heard her playing.

He had seemed so sad and she wished that she had been able to continue with the Chopin *étude*, so that he could have listened and enjoyed it, just as Papa used to do.

Her thoughts were interrupted by Lady Armstrong.

"Ethel, darling," she was saying, "Why don't you two young things take a stroll outside? Mrs. Lewis and I are so comfortable here by the fire and I am sure you don't want to listen to our silly old chatter."

"What a great idea!" Ethel cried. "We shall go and have a look around the shops, won't we, Lucilla!"

And she bustled Lucilla out into the hall and called for the parlour maid to bring her hat and coat.

"But – it's raining," Lucilla said, looking at Ethel's exquisite cream and blue dress and her matching leather shoes. "Your outfit will get splashed."

"Oh goodness, that doesn't matter!" Ethel laughed, and turned so that the parlour maid could help her into her beige woollen coat. "Now that I have Mortimer in the bag, I need never worry about such trifles again."

And she then took her large hat from the maid and peered into the hall mirror to make sure that she had the veil arranged in just the right way.

Now the parlour maid was holding up Lucilla's old navy blue velvet coat, so she could slide her arms into it.

"Oh really!" Ethel said, as she watched Lucilla put on the little velvet hat that went with her coat. "That hat is only fit for a schoolgirl. I can't walk out with you looking like that. Don't you have another?"

Lucilla shook her head forlornly, but Ethel was already stepping out of the door, so she took an umbrella from the stand by the front door and hurried after her.

The two girls picked their way between the puddles as they walked along the pavement and all the time Lucilla was trying to hold the umbrella over Ethel's hat, although she did not seem to mind that the rain was falling on it.

"We shall now go to Whiteley's Department store," Ethel announced. "I am hatching a little plan!"

Lucilla was surprised that Ethel should make such a suggestion, as she had only been to Whiteley's with her aunt once, when they had been to buy the dress she had worn to the engagement party.

The store was not far from Aunt Maud's house and was a vast square building with many floors.

As they went in through the big glass door, Lucilla looked around at all the bolts and rolls of fabric that were laid out on counters everywhere.

There were silks and satins in every colour of the rainbow and thick heavy tweeds in soft green and brown shades that reminded her of the winter colours of the fields and hedgerows that surrounded her old home.

"Come on, quickly!" Ethel seized her arm and was pulling her onwards. "You *are* an old slowcoach."

Then they found themselves in a part of the store where a group of tailor's dummies stood silently waiting, draped in velvet and wool coats.

"Good afternoon, Miss Armstrong," a stout man with hair slicked down over his forehead came to greet them. "How may I help you?"

"This young lady, as you can see, is in dire need of a new coat," Ethel replied, lifting her veil and folding it back as she smiled at Lucilla. "Do you see anything that you like?"

Lucilla's face felt warm.

What was Ethel thinking of? She could not possibly buy a new coat. She had no money of her own.

"I think this is very nice."

Ethel stroked the sleeve of a soft pink wool coat with a smart trimming of fur at the cuffs.

"Try it on!"

"No – really, I mustn't!" Lucilla stammered and was about to explain that she could not possibly afford something quite so luxurious and expensive, but the shop assistant was already lifting it down from the dummy and holding it out for her.

Ethel took hold of Lucilla's collar and pulled her old velvet coat from her back.

"Go on!" she insisted. "Try it! It's just perfect for you."

Reluctantly Lucilla slid her arms into the silk-lined sleeves of the sublime coat and then felt the luxurious soft warmth of it as she wrapped it around herself.

"Oh!"

Ethel's pale face was flushing with excitement.

"Look at that! You are transformed! The pink is a perfect match for your hair – and it makes your eyes look really blue too."

The shop assistant invited Lucilla to look at herself in a long mirror beside the display of coats.

For a moment she felt that she was staring at the reflection of someone else altogether, a proud and happy girl with a glorious mane of shining brown hair, dressed in a winter coat that looked fit for a Russian Princess.

The Princess smiled back at her, her huge blue eyes shining with delight, and then Lucilla remembered where she was and what she must do and she turned away from the mirror.

"It's very lovely," she said to the shop assistant, "but I cannot possibly afford to buy something like this. Please can I have my own coat back."

Ethel was rummaging in the silk handbag that was hanging over her arm.

"Don't be so ridiculous, Lucilla" she chided. "That coat is yours. It's absolutely made for you and it would be criminal of you to walk out of the shop without it."

Lucilla felt her cheeks turn red with embarrassment as she watched Ethel pull out a bundle of notes and count a handful of them out to give to the shop assistant.

"There," she exclaimed. "It's yours, Lucilla."

"No, no! I cannot possibly – "

Lucilla tried to pull her arms out of the lovely coat and hand it back to the shop assistant, but Ethel stopped her and held up the big bundle of money that was still left after buying the coat.

"Mortimer gave me all this yesterday to spend on whatever I liked," she crowed. "And now I've decided I want to spend it on you! I can't be seen out with someone who looks like an old ragbag."

"But what will your Mama say?"

Lucilla was desperately trying to think of some way to stop Ethel.

"It's nothing to do with her. It's between me and my fiancé!"

Ethel held her head high under her huge hat.

"But Aunt Maud might not be at all happy for me to accept such a lovely gift – "

"That silly old aunt of yours just wants to get you married off as soon as possible," Ethel told her. "I don't suppose for one minute that she will make a fuss about me buying something that makes you look so pretty."

Lucilla was confused and upset, as it seemed as if Ethel did not care how she felt at all.

"I don't know – what to say!" she whispered.

"Try 'thank you'!" Ethel smiled and told the shop assistant to put Lucilla's old coat in a bag so they could carry it with them.

"Come along, now we are going to have tea," she added when he had done so.

As they sat at a little table in the restaurant on the top floor of the department store, sipping piping hot tea and nibbling on currant buns, Lucilla decided to make the best of the situation and tried to thank Ethel for the coat.

"Oh – thank dear Mortimer, darling, if you must!"

Ethel's green eyes looked down at her plate, as if she was embarrassed.

"Is it – nice? Being engaged?" Lucilla asked after a moment.

Ethel did not look up, but concentrated on breaking up her bun into little pieces and picking out the currants.

"It's utterly marvellous," she replied. "I shall never have to ask Mama and Papa for another thing!"

"And – do you think that you will be happy with – Mortimer?"

Lucilla could not but remember how much older than Ethel the American stockbroker had seemed. Almost like an uncle, as he had bent over her hand to kiss it.

"Oh, crumbs, yes." Ethel looked up now, her green eyes glowing. "We shall have a house on Park Lane, an apartment in New York and a villa in the Italian Lakes."

"What I meant was," Lucilla continued, "will you like spending *time* with him?"

Ethel shrugged.

"I don't suppose I'll see much of him, once we are married. He'll go off and work and visit his Club. And I shall be able to get on with my own life."

Lucilla thought Ethel's face had gone a shade paler as she said this and her eyes looked bitter.

"Do you love him, Ethel?" she asked after a pause.

"Yes, of course I do! He's so kind," Ethel flashed back and she gave Lucilla a stern look. "We'll be very happy, don't you worry. And so will you, when we find a beau for you."

"I really do hope so, Ethel. I often think of Mama and Papa and how happy they were. I'm glad that – they – that the accident happened to both of them, as they would have wanted to always be together – they loved each other so much."

Her eyes stung with tears as she recalled the awful day the telegram had arrived at Wellsprings Place, telling her that Lord and Lady Welton had been killed by a sudden avalanche high in the Alps.

"Oh, love!" Ethel sighed. "Nothing but trouble, if you ask me."

She looked bitter and angry again and then began to fiddle with her currant bun once more.

"Love is the best thing in the whole world!" Lucilla cried. "I cannot imagine spending my life with someone I did not love!"

Ethel frowned at her.

"Love can be all very well," she said, "but I want money. I'll love my house in Park Lane and that will do me very nicely, thank you!"

Lucilla shivered at these words and at the cold look in Ethel's eyes.

"Haven't you ever been in love with any one?" she asked.

"Oh, yes," Ethel replied and pulled her veil down so that the spotted net hid her eyes. "And much good it did me. Come along, Missy, let's go and show your aunt what we found for you at Whiteley's!"

*

Aunt Maud and Lady Armstrong were sitting very comfortably by the fire when the two girls returned and, much to Lucilla's surprise, her aunt just smiled when she saw the new coat.

"How very kind!" she purred at Ethel, "and you are very thoughtful to my niece."

Lady Armstrong nodded in agreement.

"Absolutely," she added. "Just what Lucilla needs. A good example for her. She will be following in Ethel's footsteps before too long, never fear!"

"Let's hope so," Aunt Maud replied. "Thank you so much, dear Lady Armstrong, for your help and advice. I shall act upon it without delay."

Lucilla felt a strange sense of unease as she heard this, but she was tired by the afternoon's shopping and was longing to go to her room and rest, so she did not stop to think what her aunt might have meant by these words.

As she lay on her bed, gazing at her beautiful pink coat on a chair, she suddenly wished that the young man with the brown eyes could see her wearing it.

'It's just the sort of look he might like,' she thought to herself. 'He would notice me, if I was dressed like a Russian Princess. After all, he wanted to hear me play Chopin – '

And then she told herself not to be so silly.

She did not know anything about him, not even his name.

And – had not she heard him talking about Ethel? Could it be that he and Ethel had once – been in love?

She must stop thinking about him, for she had only met him for just a few moments and he had not taken any notice of her at all.

'I will find someone to love,' she told herself. 'If I am patient, I know it will happen. It happened to Mama and Papa and it *will* happen for me!'

But the young man was still in her mind and she could not stop herself thinking about him all that evening.

*

The next day, Aunt Maud went down to the kitchen and spent a very long time in consultation with the cook.

When she finally came back to the drawing room, where Lucilla was busy darning an old petticoat, she then announced that she was holding a dinner party that very evening.

"A very dear friend of mine, a Mr. Pargetter, will be joining us," she said, her cheeks reddening as she spoke. "And a second gentleman, too, an acquaintance of your new friend, Ethel, will make up the quartet."

Lucilla's heart leapt in her breast.

Ethel must have spoken to the dark-eyed young man and it was he who would be coming to dinner!

Never mind that he had been upset and angry and he had not wanted to dance with her at the party. Now he had thought better of it and Ethel had persuaded him to come and visit her.

"I'm glad to see you looking so cheerful," Aunt Maud commented, "and I am sure I don't need to tell you that you must look your best this evening. Though I must remind you to devote yourself to the young man Ethel is introducing. Mr. Pargetter is *my* guest and he has come to see *me*. I don't want you trying to attract his attention."

Lucilla remembered what she had overheard her aunt saying to Lady Armstrong.

And she had no intention of trying to distract Mr. Pargetter, whoever he might be.

All her conversation and all her attention would be devoted to the dark-eyed young man and the very thought of seeing him again made her feel as light and joyful as a butterfly.

She took a long time to get ready that evening.

It was a shame that she had only one evening dress, the pale-blue silk she had worn to the party, as she would have liked the young man to see her in something different when they met again.

Then she had an idea.

Among the few things Lucilla had brought with her from Wellsprings Place was a peacock blue stole that had belonged to her Mama.

She threw it around her shoulders and then tied her brown hair into a loose knot, for, as well as being the very latest fashion, this showed off her abundant shining tresses to their best advantage.

She looked in the mirror and there, once more, was the Russian Princess, draped in brilliant blue with her mass of hair framing her delicate face.

Downstairs in the hall she could hear the front door opening and the sound of voices and she knew that it was almost time for her to go down.

Lucilla did not wait for her aunt to send the parlour maid to call her.

Her feet scarcely touched the floor as she ran down the stairs.

Aunt Maud was standing by the fire, talking to a large gentleman with a shining bald head.

Lucilla could only see his back view, but she at once realised that it must be Mr. Pargetter.

She stepped into the room, remembering to keep her eyes down and to behave in as modest and mouse-like manner as she could, as she knew that she must not attract Mr. Pargetter's attention or her aunt would be angry.

"My niece, Lady Lucilla Welton," Aunt Maud said.

Lucilla curtsied politely, keeping her gaze fixed on the hearthrug.

"Good evening, Lucilla," the man responded in an American accent.

Lucilla felt her hand taken in a strong clasp, as the man reached out and raised her fingers to his lips.

She tried to draw back, confused, as she had not expected her aunt's friend to be an American, but his grip on her hand was too strong for her to escape.

"Mr. Pargetter – " she began, suddenly feeling very afraid.

"So, we meet again," the man said. "You're lookin' swell, Princess."

Horrified, Lucilla looked up to find herself face to face with Harkness Jackson.

She had forgotten all about him, but now that she saw him again, she remembered how much she had hated dancing with him and how unpleasant it had been to feel his hand clutching at her waist.

'How could I have been so stupid?' she thought. 'Why ever did I think that Ethel would send that young man with the sad expression? He was her beau once and anyway why would he remember me?'

There was a commotion in the hall and Aunt Maud hurried out of the room.

It must be Mr. Pargetter arriving, Lucilla thought.

Harkness Jackson squeezed her hand a little more tightly and pulled her towards him.

"So now, my Princess. Have you missed me?" he whispered and Lucilla caught the smell of whisky on his breath.

She was saved from having to reply by the return of her aunt, followed by a short gentleman wearing very thick spectacles with round rims.

Aunt Maud's eyes were bright and her face flushed, as if she had been sitting much too close to the fire.

"Well – we are all gathered, we may as well go in to dinner," she intoned, sounding a little out of breath.

Harkness passed the tip of his tongue over his lips.

"Great," he chuckled. "I'm as hungry as a horse."

And he slid Lucilla's hand under his arm and pulled her even closer to him as they walked into the dining room after Aunt Maud and Mr. Pargetter.

CHAPTER THREE

Harkness Jackson raised one of Aunt Maud's best wine glasses and looked at Lucilla.

"A toast to you, Princess!" he drawled and drained the wine from his glass in one draught.

'How dare he call me Princess!' Lucilla thought, looking down at her plate and wishing she was anywhere but at her aunt's dinner table.

She might have thought herself a Russian Princess, when she wore the beautiful coat and when she wrapped the brilliant blue stole around her shoulders, but that was something very private.

Something she only wanted to share with a person she liked, someone just like the young man she had met at Ethel's engagement party.

"Would you care for more beef, Mr. Jackson," Aunt Maud asked, as the American's plate was empty already, even though everyone else had hardly begun to eat.

"Sure!"

The bald American shoved his plate towards her.

"I've one hell of an appetite this evening, ma'am."

"Hoskins will serve you, Mr. Jackson, if you wait just one moment," Aunt Maud said, looking rather put out, and she rang the little silver bell to call the housekeeper.

"Ah, manners, manners! Pardon me, ma'am, your kind hospitality makes me feel so at home that I clean forgot 'em!"

Mr. Jackson helped himself to some more wine and raised his glass to Aunt Maud.

Mrs. Hoskins, the housekeeper, came quietly into the dining room and loaded his plate with vegetables and gravy, while Mr. Pargetter, who was sitting at the head of the table, carved some thin slices from the joint of beef.

"Don't be shy, there, sir!" Mr. Jackson chortled. "Remember I'm from Texas! I was raised on beef steaks!"

Mr. Pargetter glanced briefly at Aunt Maud through his round glasses and cut a few more thin slices for Mr. Jackson.

As soon as they were on his plate, the American speared one of the slices of beef and popped it whole into his mouth.

"It's good," he mumbled, chewing away, "but it's not as good as the meat from my Texas Longhorns. I look forward, ma'am, to the day when you and Lady Lucilla sit down for dinner at Jackson's Drift and I'll have my sister cook prime ribs and pumpkin pie for you!"

"How very kind," Aunt Maud sniffed, watching as Mr. Jackson devoured his plate of roast beef.

"Hoskins – will you bring another bottle of wine? Mr. Jackson's glass is empty."

There was a short silence as Mr. Jackson went to work on the rest of the food on his plate.

Then Mr. Pargetter spoke up.

"You are very quiet, young Lucilla. Is something wrong?"

Lucilla shook her head and tried to make herself smile.

"Hey, Princess! Eat up." Mr. Jackson intervened. "It may not be Texan, but it's still beef, and it'll put those English roses back in your cheeks!"

Lucilla picked up her knife and fork and tried very hard to make herself eat some of the food in front of her, but she was not at all hungry.

She felt that she could not possibly eat with Mr. Harkness Jackson sitting opposite her, staring at her with his greedy little eyes.

Aunt Maud snorted and looked as if she was about to say something, but instead she picked up her napkin and dabbed at her lips.

"That blue is a very charming colour on you," Mr. Pargetter was now saying. "It brings out the colour of your eyes quite perfectly, Lucilla."

Harkness Jackson laughed.

"You took the words right out of my mouth, sir! Ain't she just the cutest little thing?"

"I agree," Mr. Pargetter simpered. "Delightful."

"Hoskins, would you clear the plates and bring in the dessert?" Aunt Maud ordered in a cold voice.

Lucilla could tell that her aunt was becoming angry and perhaps Mr. Pargetter too had noticed that something was amiss, as he turned to Aunt Maud and refilled her wine glass.

Mr. Jackson just carried on talking.

"These English girls are the prettiest I've seen," he was saying. "My good friend, Mortimer, has just gotten himself hitched to one of them and I'm thinkin' I could do a lot worse that follow in his footsteps – "

Lucilla felt herself turn hot and cold as she heard these words.

Surely he could not mean that she, Lucilla, might ever consider him as a husband?

Hoskins was now placing small dishes of meringue with raspberry sauce and cream in front of the diners.

"Lucilla, whatever is the matter with you?" Aunt Maud admonished her sharply. "Do stop picking at your food."

Although meringues were normally one of Lucilla's favourite desserts, she could do no more than break them up with her fork and move them round her plate.

"She does look awfully pale, Maud." Mr. Pargetter said. "Perhaps she is sickening for something."

And he coughed and raised his napkin to his face as if trying to ward off any germs that might be emanating from Lucilla.

"Well? Lucilla?" Aunt Maud asked, frowning at her niece. "Is there something wrong?"

Harkness Jackson was getting to his feet.

"Nothin' that a drop of this won't cure!" he cried, as he came around the table to Lucilla and, picking up her wineglass, held it to her lips.

Lucilla thought that she might faint if she had to taste the wine and she could not bear it that he was now touching the back of her head with one of his large hands, as he urged her to drink.

"I am so sorry," she murmured, trying to lean away from him, "but I have a terrible headache. I wonder – if I might be excused?"

Aunt Maud's lips became a thin line, as if she was trying to hold everything she wanted to say inside herself.

"Of course, my dear," she said, after a moment, in a cold voice. "If you are unwell, you must go to your room. But what a shame that Mr. Jackson has troubled to come all this way to visit us and find you indisposed."

Mr. Jackson patted Lucilla's head.

"Poor Princess. I'll just have to come back another day."

And he stroked Lucilla's hair, sending cold shivers down her spine.

"I am sorry, but you must excuse me – I am not feeling at all well," Lucilla persisted, her voice little more than a whisper.

"You have permission to go to your room," Aunt Maud said coldly. "And, if Mr. Jackson is able to forgive your rudeness, perhaps we will have the pleasure of seeing him here again, when you are feeling better."

"Why, of course!" Mr. Jackson piped up. "I should be delighted to call on you and your lovely niece, ma'am. In the meantime, Pargetter, how's about a game of cards?"

Lucilla rose to her feet and ducked away from the American's heavy hand that was still resting on her head. Mr. Pargetter was looking nervous at the prospect of facing Mr. Jackson at cards and Aunt Maud's face was rigid with disapproval.

If Lucilla had not been feeling quite so unhappy, she might have found the little scene round the dinner table quite amusing, but now all she could think of was escaping to the peace and safety of her bedroom.

She did not bother to turn up the gaslight, but lay down straight away on her bed and buried her hot cheeks in the cool soft pillow.

But even now that she was alone, her heart beat fast with anxiety.

What was it Mr. Jackson had said?

That his friend Mortimer had just *'got hitched'* to an English girl and that he, Harkness Jackson, *'could do worse that follow in his footsteps –'*

His words echoed round and round in her head and she then remembered the way he had gazed at her as he said them, his little grey eyes eating up her face.

There was only one explanation for his presence at the dinner table.

He was looking for an English bride, preferably one with a title and he had then decided that she, Lady Lucilla Welton, was the one.

'No one could ever expect me to marry someone like that,' she thought to herself. 'Even Aunt Maud, who wants to be rid of me, must be able to see how ridiculous he is.'

She held onto this thought, as it was a comforting one and after a little while, she found herself drifting off into sleep.

*

The next morning, Lucilla ate her porridge all on her own, as Aunt Maud did not come down to breakfast.

"Mrs. Lewis is indisposed," Hoskins informed her, as she poured weak tea into Lucilla's cup. "She has a bad head and is resting."

Lucilla wondered how the rest of the dinner party had gone and whether or not Mr. Jackson had beaten Mr. Pargetter at cards, but she did not like to ask, as Hoskins was looking far from cheerful.

The servants always had a lot of extra work when Aunt Maud took it upon herself to entertain.

Lucilla had just finished her porridge, which she ate without thinking this morning, as she was so hungry and she was just sipping a cup of tea, when Hoskins returned carrying a small silver tray.

"This came for you, my Lady," she said and she held out the tray on which a large pink envelope lay.

"For me?"

Lucilla was surprised, as she had never yet received any mail during her stay at Aunt Maud's.

"Delivered by hand just a moment ago, my Lady," Hoskins added.

And there, written on the brown envelope in a large flowing hand, was Lucilla's name.

Inside on pink paper was a short note in the same bold handwriting,

"Dear Lucilla,

I can't wait to hear how you got on last night! Why don't you come to ours this morning and we can have a good gossip? You can even use the piano if you like, no one else does here and you play so well.

Yours,

Ethel. "

Once again, Lucilla was surprised.

Why was Ethel being so friendly to her, when they hardly knew each other?

She was not at all sure if she really liked Ethel, as the purchase of the beautiful pink coat still made her feel very uncomfortable. She really did not want Ethel to do anything like that again.

On the other hand, the idea of being able to play the wonderful piano at Lord and Lady Armstrong's house was most appealing.

"Do you think that my aunt would mind if I went out this morning?" she asked Hoskins.

Hoskins put her head on one side.

"I wouldn't care to say, my Lady."

"Oh, never mind, Hoskins. I will stay here. Perhaps my aunt will need me to help her with something, if she is feeling unwell."

"Indeed, my Lady," Hoskins replied. "Will you be taking your tea through to the parlour this morning?"

The housekeeper looked pointedly at Lucilla's empty porridge bowl.

"Yes, of course, Hoskins. I shall. You may clear the table."

Lucilla carried her cup and saucer into the parlour and sat by the empty fireplace.

The fire had not been lit this morning due to Aunt Maud's indisposition and the room was feeling chilly.

'I wonder why Ethel is taking such an interest in me?' she thought. 'For I am not really part of her Social circle.'

She was just trying to decide whether she should take up Ethel's offer of playing the Armstrong's wonderful grand piano, when there was a sharp knock at the front door.

For one awful moment, Lucilla thought that it was Harkness Jackson come to call on her.

Then the parlour door opened and Hoskins showed Mr. Pargetter into the room.

The little man smiled at Lucilla, peering at her over the top of his round glasses as he sat down on the chair, which faced hers.

"Why, what an unexpected pleasure, Lucilla!" he exclaimed. "I trust you are feeling better this morning?"

"Indeed I am, thank you, Mr. Pargetter. I am afraid it is my poor aunt who is under the weather today. She will be so disappointed to have missed you."

"I am sorry to hear she is unwell."

Mr. Pargetter coughed and Lucilla noticed that his cheeks were turning pink.

"But – I cannot say that I am not delighted to have you all to myself."

Lucilla did not know quite what to say.

Mr. Pargetter was staring at her in a very odd way.

"Lucilla," he started with a quiver in his voice. "The colour has come back into your cheeks and, I have to say, you are looking extraordinarily lovely."

"Please, Mr. Pargetter, there is no need – "

Lucilla rose to her feet, as she knew that she should not stay in the room while he was speaking to her like this.

"Oh, but there is every need. You poor sweet child, I did feel such sympathy for you yesterday, suffering the attentions of that brutish American fellow. If you could only know how it pained me to see the way he laid his coarse hands on your beautiful hair – "

To Lucilla's utter horror, Mr. Pargetter had leapt to his feet and caught one of her tresses in his stubby fingers.

"Dearest little Lucilla," he muttered and raised the tress to his lips.

Lucilla froze instantly to the spot, as she saw, over his shoulder, that Aunt Maud had come downstairs and was watching them from the doorway.

Her face was white with anger.

"Lucilla," she called out, her eyes like chips of ice. "What are you doing?"

Mr. Pargetter dropped the strand of Lucilla's hair as if it was burning his fingers.

"Maud, my dear! You are – feeling better!"

"Oh, yes," Aunt Maud replied, still glaring at Lucilla. "I am feeling quite well now. I should like a private word with my niece, Mr. Pargetter, and then I shall be delighted to entertain you for coffee. Lucilla, will you come with me?"

Lucilla's legs were trembling, but she followed her aunt out of the parlour and into the dining room, which still smelt faintly of roast beef from the night before.

The moment the door was closed behind them, Aunt Maud raised her hand and Lucilla felt a stinging blow on the side of her face.

"You despicable creature!" Aunt Maud screamed. "So this is how you repay my generosity! Now I can see exactly what I have been harbouring in my house these last months."

Lucilla's head was spinning from the blow.

She had never been hit before in her entire life and the shock of it, as much as the pain, made her feel giddy.

"I am very sorry, Aunt," she whispered, holding her hand to her cheek. "I did not mean – "

She wanted to say that it was not her fault that Mr. Pargetter had taken her by surprise, but somehow she knew that this would only make Aunt Maud even angrier.

"Get out!" her aunt was shouting now. "I will not have you in this house when I am entertaining the man I intend to marry. Get out! And don't come back until you have repented of your shocking behaviour."

Lucilla ran up to her room, struggling to hold back the tears that were welling up in her eyes.

As she threw herself down on her bed, she realised that she was still holding Ethel's note in her hand.

'I will go there,' she thought, 'as there is no one else I can turn to. I don't really like Ethel, but I have nowhere else to go!'

And then, unexpectedly, she found herself thinking of the young man with the brown eyes. The last time she had seen him was at Lady Armstrong's and somehow she could not help but wonder if he might be there again.

'I should so like to see him and speak to him and find out why he looks so sad,' she mused and she found that her tears were drying up and her spirits had lifted just a little.

41

'I must look my best,' she told herself and she put on her blue-and-white dress with the ruffled sleeves and then over it, the wonderful pink coat Ethel had bought for her.

Then she ran downstairs, not daring to speak to her aunt again, who was now with Mr. Pargetter in the parlour and let herself out into the crisp and cold morning air.

*

When Lucilla arrived at Lady Armstrong's mansion, Ethel came running into the hall to greet her.

"Oh, good. It's you, Lucilla. Mama is out and I'm going quite mad with nobody to talk to."

She ushered Lucilla into the cream-painted parlour, which was very light and airy due to the large windows that faced out over the street.

"I've already rung for coffee," she said, "so sit down and you can tell me all about last night."

"There is very little to tell," Lucilla began, as the parlour maid offered her a china cup full of delicious coffee and added cream and sugar – two items rarely seen in Aunt Maud's household.

"But Ethel, I have upset my aunt quite dreadfully."

She explained to Ethel what had happened and Ethel burst out laughing.

"She slapped you? Oh, that is the funniest thing I have heard for ages! I can't wait to tell Mama!"

"It – is not very funny for me."

Lucilla found Ethel's laughter very unkind and she struggled to keep back the tears that welled up in her eyes as she remembered how angry her aunt had been.

"It must have hurt, for I can still see a red mark on your face. But really, Lucilla, you should just have slapped her right back. I would have done."

Ethel was still laughing at her.

"Anyway, you must tell me about last night. What happened? Harkness was over the moon when your aunt invited him!"

"I had a bad headache at dinner," Lucilla explained, "and I had to go to bed early."

"You're making a habit of it!"

Ethel was frowning now.

"You will never get anywhere, Missy, if you keep leaving the fray at the crucial moment."

"Oh, I am sure Mr. Jackson did not mind too much. He was going to play cards with Mr. Pargetter."

Ethel struck her forehead in a gesture of despair.

"Lucilla, you are such a fool. Harkness is absolutely crazy for you. He talks about nothing else. And do you know how much money he has? If I wasn't already engaged to Mortimer – "

"Please, Ethel, stop!" Lucilla cried. "You just don't understand – Mr. Jackson is not someone I could ever think of in that way."

Ethel leaned forward in her chair, her green eyes very bright.

"Lucilla, you must be sensible. You cannot go on living with your aunt forever."

"I may not be able to go on living with her at all after today," Lucilla commented sadly.

"Well – what does that matter? You have a beau, Lucilla! A rich American, who would marry you at the drop of a hat."

"I am sure that even my aunt would not want me to marry someone like that, who I don't even know."

Ethel raised her blonde eyebrows.

"I wouldn't bet on it. Oh, Lucilla, what's wrong with you? You are such a pretty girl and good company too. Just think what fun we could have if you married Harkness! He and Mortimer are the best of friends – why, we could see each other all the time and we would never have to worry how much we were spending!"

"Ethel – please!" Lucilla cried. "You must stop!"

She could not hold back her tears any longer and they were running down her cheeks.

Ethel seemed to have no idea how much she disliked Harkness Jackson.

"Oh, I'm sorry," Ethel said after a moment. "Mama always tells me how bossy I am! Let's forget it for now. Why don't you come and play the piano? There's no one at home now except for us and you can play away to your heart's content."

Lucilla was feeling decidedly uneasy about Ethel's remarks.

Could she really mean that she thought it would be a good idea for her to marry Harkness Jackson? Could she not see how much she hated the American?

But it was Heaven to sit down at the grand piano again in the little salon and as Lucilla felt the smooth ivory keys beneath her fingers, her troubled thoughts vanished.

She started with a few soft notes and then just let the music flow right through her, as she found herself playing another of her Papa's favourite Chopin waltzes.

Ethel sat close by on one of the gilt chairs, but she could not stay still for long.

After a while she stood up and put her handkerchief to her eyes.

"You play so beautifully, but don't you know any cheerful tunes?" she asked, as Lucilla picked out the closing notes of the waltz.

Before Lucilla could reply, there was a commotion from the street outside and Ethel ran to see what was going on.

"Lucilla, quick!" she shrieked. "You have to come and see this!"

The two girls peered down from the window and Lucilla could see a strange contraption that looked rather like a carriage without its horses and it was belching smoke and making a loud grinding noise.

Seated on the weird contraption there were two gentlemen wearing leather hats, goggles and thick glasses.

"How amazing! Mortimer's gone and done it!" Ethel sighed. "He's bought a motor car!"

"Oh – so that's what it is then!" Lucilla said, remembering that she had seen similar contraptions on several occasions, when she had been out in London with her aunt.

She watched from the window as the two gentlemen tinkered about with its engine until the grinding noise and the smoke stopped.

Then her heart sank as the larger of the two pulled off his hat and goggles and she could see that he was Harkness Jackson.

"Ethel, thank you very much for the coffee and the piano, but I should be thinking about leaving," she began, trying to ignore the feeling of despair that overcame her as she thought of returning to her aunt's house.

Ethel smiled mischievously.

"Too late, Lucilla!" she cried out. "Look – they're coming in!"

Lucilla turned back to the piano and tried to play again, but her fingers had turned numb and useless and she might just as well have tried to pick out a tune with boxing gloves on.

With a great clatter of boots on the parquet floor and a loud roar of laughter, Harkness and Mortimer came into the salon.

"Did you see it, honey?" Mortimer was shouting to Ethel. "What did you think? Isn't she a beauty?"

"Well, I don't know about all that smoke – and what a frightful racket!" Ethel said, as Mortimer clasped her in a bear hug.

"Hey, Princess!"

Harkness was coming towards Lucilla, looking rather like a large frog, she thought, with his wide shiny face and his tightly buttoned green motoring coat.

"How is the girl, today?"

"Oh dear!" Ethel called out, extricating herself from Mortimer's arms. "She is in need of rescuing, Harkness. That awful old aunt of hers has been on the warpath."

Harkness came over to Lucilla and dropped heavily on his knees next to the piano stool.

There was *nowhere* for Lucilla to escape to.

He was just too big for her to slip past and, anyway, Mortimer and Ethel were blocking the way through the door.

Harkness seized Lucilla's hand in his large ones and held it so tightly that she winced with pain.

"Princess," he breathed heavily, his little grey eyes staring into hers and Lucilla felt her heart turn to stone as she heard him say, "look no further. I am your man."

CHAPTER FOUR

Lucilla looked desperately towards Ethel, wishing that she might say something to make Harkness Jackson leave her alone.

But Ethel just smiled and then nodded her elegant blonde head, as if she had been planning this meeting all along.

"Come along, Mortimer dear," she cooed. "I don't think we are very welcome here just at the moment."

"Aha!" he exclaimed, gazing at his friend Harkness, still on his knees in front of Lucilla. "Sure, honey, let's go."

And the two of them left Lucilla alone in the salon, her hand caught in the big American's grasp.

"Please, will you let me go?" Lucilla begged him, struggling to keep her voice steady.

"Lady Lucilla," Harkness began, clutching her hand even tighter. "Princess! I was all set to call on you this afternoon – but you have come to me instead!"

"I – didn't know that you would be here," Lucilla managed to say, "I came to visit Ethel – "

Harkness was not listening.

"From the first moment I set eyes on you," he was saying, "I knew you were the girl for me. I've waited a long time to find a wife and now I've found her. I ain't goin' to beat about the bush. What do you say, Lucilla? Will you be mine? "

Lucilla closed her eyes as a wave of fear passed through her body.

"No!" she managed to say at last. "No, I can't!"

To her horror she heard Harkness laughing.

"Atta girl!" he chortled. "I like a girl with spirit. A *lady* with spirit, even better!"

"Please Mr. Jackson, I am quite serious!" Lucilla cried.

"Ah, so am I, Princess." Harkness raised her hand and kissed it. "I've never been so serious in all my life."

"So then, Mr. Jackson, you must listen to me! I cannot possibly accept your proposal of marriage – "

He lowered her hand and gazed at her admiringly with his little grey eyes.

Then he grinned.

"Ah – I know what you're up to! You're playin' hard to get!"

"No, no, I am not!" Lucilla's voice cracked as she tried desperately to make him listen. "Please, believe me, I cannot marry you."

Harkness let go of her hand.

He shook his head and sat back on his heels.

"You look adorable, Princess. Them roses in your cheeks are comin' right into bloom. I'm goin' to let you play your little game with me, sweetheart, for I know that girls love to say 'no' when they mean 'yes'."

Lucilla tried to think of some other words she could use to make him understand that she meant what she was saying and that she could never, never become his wife.

But before she could speak, there was a tap at the door of the salon and Ethel came in.

"Well?" she enquired, tossing her blonde head and smiling brightly, "can I congratulate you?"

Harkness chuckled.

"I'm gettin' a rough ride – this cute little English rose is turnin' out to be a bit of a wild mustang. But – I like 'em fiery and I'm stickin' with this one till she gives in."

"Lucilla!" Ethel exclaimed, looking cross, "How can you be so hard-hearted! Dear old Harkness – " she patted the American's bald head as she said this, " – is completely besotted with you. How can you be such a tease?"

"I'm not – really not – being a tease!"

"Oh, you English girls!"

Harkness climbed to his feet, leaning on Ethel's shoulder, as he was rather stiff now from kneeling down for so long.

"So straight-laced and yet so fiery, all at the same time. I just adore you, gorgeous."

"Why don't you go now and sit with Mortimer, Harkness, and have some coffee? You must have lots of things to discuss after all that business with the motor car," Ethel suggested, "and leave Lucilla to me for a moment."

The American shrugged and went out of the little salon, leaving the two of them alone.

Lucilla took a deep breath, as she felt as if all the time the big man had been with her in the salon, there had been no air at all and then she took out her handkerchief and wiped her hand where he had kissed it.

"Well?" Ethel's green eyes were piercingly bright. "Did he propose?"

Lucilla nodded, not trusting herself to speak.

"But you turned him down?"

Lucilla nodded again.

Ethel sat on one of the little chairs with a heavy frown wrinkling her brow.

"Well. All may not yet be lost," she said after a moment. "It hasn't made him like you any the less – in fact, I think he's even keener, if that's possible."

"Ethel – I don't want to marry him! I couldn't!" Lucilla cried, finding her voice at last.

"Don't be ridiculous, Lucilla. Just think, we could have a double wedding. Mortimer and me – and you and Harkness! We would be the talk of London. It would be the Society event of the year!"

Now her green eyes glowed with excitement.

"But – I'm sorry, Ethel – I can't!"

Lucilla now struggled to hold back her tears.

"I'm sure you'll come round to the idea in the end." Ethel sighed. "After all, what other options do you have? Do you really think you can go back to Mrs. Lewis's?"

Lucilla wiped her eyes and then touched her cheek, where her aunt had slapped her.

It still felt very tender.

"I have nowhere else to go," she murmured.

"Why don't you stay here with me for a while and think it all over? I know Mama won't mind as she likes you."

"I – should leave, now – "

The mere thought of staying with Lord and Lady Armstrong where Harkness Jackson was likely to return and bother her at any moment, filled Lucilla with dread.

But then she could see her aunt's angry face and the horrid cold house, where she had felt so unhappy and tears welled up in her eyes again.

Ethel sighed impatiently.

"Well – I suppose if you do go back to your aunt's, it might help you to see sense. Mortimer and I will come with you, Lucilla, if you like. We could drive you in the new motor car!"

"No, it's quite all right – I can easily walk," Lucilla replied quickly, as she thought that Ethel might well ask Harkness Jackson too and she most certainly did not want to have to sit next to him.

"Don't be silly," Ethel scolded her. "Your aunt will not be half as unpleasant to you if I come with you. I will ring for our coats!"

In the event Harkness Jackson did not come with them in the car – although he wanted to – but there were not enough hats and goggles to go around and, as it was such a cold day with a North wind blowing, he then insisted that Lucilla borrow his, to protect her face from the weather.

"Be seein' you, Princess," he almost shouted, as he helped Lucilla up the steep step into the motor car. "Keep them pretty roses bloomin' for me!"

She hated the feel of the goggles against her face, knowing that, only a very short while before, *he* had been wearing them.

But at least he was not there sitting beside her, she reflected, as the motor car roared into life and rattled away down the street, leaving Harkness waving to them from the pavement.

Lucilla felt quite faint as the car pulled up outside Aunt Maud's house, as her nose was full of the fumes from the engine and her ears were ringing with the noise.

Aunt Maud came out of the house and was standing on the front steps, her face a picture of astonishment as she gazed at the motor car.

Ethel pulled off her goggles and called out to her,

"Good morning, Mrs. Lewis! We've just brought Lucilla back."

Aunt Maud now looked even more surprised, as she watched while Lucilla removed her goggles and shook out her hair that had been flattened by Harkness's leather hat.

"What – what?" she stammered.

"I shan't come in," Ethel called, "but I think Lucilla has some news to tell you that will make you very happy, Mrs. Lewis!"

"Ethel, don't!" Lucilla cried. "Don't tell her!"

"Foolish girl!" Ethel whispered, leaning close to Lucilla. "I bet you'll think better of refusing Harkness just as soon as you walk through that front door. And, Lucilla, just picture that double wedding! I'm counting on you – we're going to be the sensation of the year!"

With that she pushed Lucilla out of the car and onto the pavement, as Mortimer revved the engine and turned in a tight circle to begin their return journey.

"I did not expect to see you so soon," Aunt Maud remarked very coldly and she stepped backwards as Lucilla came through the door and into the hall, as if she found her niece most distasteful.

"I am sorry for what happened this morning, Aunt, but it was not my fault. I did not know that Mr. Pargetter was expected or I would not have stayed downstairs."

Aunt Maud sniffed.

"You know my feelings on the matter. I cannot have you under my roof when my fiancé comes to visit."

"Oh, I didn't know. Congratulations, Aunt Maud!"

"Yes, Mr. Pargetter proposed to me this morning, Lucilla. We are to be married in a month. Arrangements must be made for you to live elsewhere, for I will not be able to offer you my hospitality any longer."

Lucilla felt her heart turn to ice as she heard this.

"I have – nowhere to go, Aunt," she mumbled.

"You should have thought of that before you took it upon yourself to behave so disgracefully. But what was Lady Armstrong's daughter shouting about just now from the seat of that extraordinary carriage?"

"Oh, it is nothing, Aunt."

"I distinctly heard her say that you had something to tell me."

"No – really – "

"If you persist in being so underhand and devious, Lucilla, I shall call on Lady Armstrong this afternoon and find out from her just what is going on."

Aunt Maud's mouth closed like a trap after these words and Lucilla knew that she would do exactly as she threatened.

"I – received a proposal of marriage – but – " she began, and saw her aunt's eyebrows rise in astonishment.

"Really, Lucilla? From whom?"

"From – Mr. Jackson. But – I did not accept."

Aunt Maud's eyebrows descended into a ferocious frown.

"What? You received an offer of marriage from a gentleman, who, I am told, is in possession of considerable wealth – and you turned it down? You little fool!"

Lucilla winced as she saw her aunt's hand rise in the air, but this time there was no slap, though her cheeks were trembling with rage as she continued speaking,

"How dare you think that you can reject such an opportunity, while you continue to not only eat me out of house and home, but in addition try to come between me and my intended husband?"

"I did not – " Lucilla began.

Aunt Maud was wringing her hands together as if in an attempt to stop herself from hitting Lucilla again.

"I am so sorry, Aunt. I really cannot marry him, I just can't – I don't like him – not at all."

"Lucilla," Aunt Maud exclaimed, slowly biting her lip to calm herself. "Go to your room. I will give you until tomorrow morning to think about your situation. If you decide to accept Mr. Jackson's proposal, you may remain here until your wedding. If you persist in behaving like a selfish little fool, you must then pack your bags and leave tomorrow."

"Thank you, Aunt," Lucilla whispered and made her way to her bedroom, her feet feeling heavy as lead as she climbed the stairs.

Alone at last, Lucilla lay down on her bed and gave way to the tears that had been threatening to overcome her ever since Harkness had proposed to her.

'How could my aunt be so cruel?' she whispered, her words lost in the feather pillow where she had hidden her face. 'She is my Mama's sister, and – my dear Mama was the kindest gentlest person!'

She could not understand it.

It seemed as if her happy childhood at Wellsprings Place and the love she had shared with her dear Mama and Papa were just a make-believe, a happy dream that was all over and finished for ever.

Lucilla now found herself living in a very different world, a place where no one seemed to understand her or care about her.

'Ethel is no friend of mine. All she really cares

about is money and clothes, and fine houses,' she thought to herself. 'I could never be like that – '

But, as her sobbing slowed and she became calmer, Lucilla began to think about what her future might hold.

Her aunt's cruelty had shocked her deeply and she could still feel the bruise on her cheek where she had been slapped.

"I cannot stay here, I cannot!" she shouted at the ceiling, sitting up and drying her eyes. 'I don't even want to spend another night here – but – what can I do?'

Perhaps, after all, she should take Ethel's advice.

Would it really be so bad to be married to someone like Harkness Jackson?

Lucilla shivered at the thought of it, and yet – he had seemed to care for her and perhaps, just like Mortimer would do for Ethel, he would buy a house for her and she could live there and not see him very often.

"No, no! I can't do it!" she cried out loud again, remembering how he had crushed her hand in his, as he knelt at her feet in the salon. 'I cannot spend the rest of my life with that man and never know – what it is – to love!'

She jumped up from her bed.

'I will now pack my bag,' she said to herself, 'and tomorrow, I shall leave this house, as Aunt Maud wants me to do and never come back here. I will then find a job as a Governess or even as a maid, if I have to, as anything will be better than to marry that man, however rich he may be!'

She found the old leather valise she had brought with her from Wellsprings Place and began to put some of her clothes into it.

Not the elegant new clothes she had acquired since she had come to London, but the familiar worn dresses she had brought with her.

Her head was full of anxieties, chasing each other round and round like a squirrel on a treadmill.

'What shall I do for money?' she thought over and over again.

If only she had her Mama's jewels, the rubies and sapphires that had looked so exquisite round her slim neck, when she went out to the theatre or the opera with Papa.

But Mama had taken all the family jewellery to Switzerland with her Papa and no one had found out what had become of it after they were killed so tragically.

Lucilla sighed as she thought of that sad painful time.

Then she remembered that there was a little pocket inside the valise for keeping valuables in and she searched inside it, hoping that perhaps she might have left some money in there in those happy days when she had joined Mama and Papa on some of their trips abroad.

Her heart leapt as her fingers met the crackle of a piece of paper.

But it was not a pound note, it was a creased and torn envelope with a folded sheet of paper hidden inside it.

"Oh, my Goodness!" Lucilla cried, as she unfolded the paper and saw the spidery writing that covered it.

In the upset and confusion of leaving Wellsprings Place, she had forgotten all about the letter that had come to her from Nanny Grove, the old woman who had looked after her and loved her when she was a small child.

Now she felt her heart turning over as she read the kind words of sympathy and condolence once again.

"My dearest Lucilla,

My heart goes out to you at this time, for it would be hard enough to lose one parent – but you have suffered the terrible loss of both your darling Mama and your dear

*Papa on the same day, and I know how dearly they loved
you and how much you will miss them.*

*I wish I could be with you, dear Lucilla, but I have
not been well and, alas, I am confined to the Cottage now
and would not be able to make the journey.*

*But you will know that my kindest thoughts are with
you and I hope that you will be strong and brave and trust
in God and in Providence to keep you safe through this
difficult time.*

Your most affectionate and loving,

Nanny Grove."

Lucilla clutched the crumpled piece of paper to her
heart and gave a cry of joy, as to read this little note made
her feel as if the old lady had come to her and given her a
tender loving hug.

'How could I have forgotten you, Nanny? I'm so
sorry, but it was all so difficult – there was so much to do
and I was so upset that I did not even reply to your letter!'

Nanny Grove had written an address at the very top
of the note, "*Holly Cottage, Ferndean, Hampshire*" and, as
Lucilla gazed at this, she suddenly knew what she must do.

Lucilla would go and visit Nanny Grove.

If the old lady was still unwell, she could look after
her and run all her errands for her.

And talking to Nanny would help her to work out
what her next step might be, as Nanny could always see a
way around any problem.

She folded up the note, stowed it back inside the
pocket of the valise and completed her packing.

Then, exhausted from her difficult morning, she lay
down on the bed and slept right through the afternoon and
all through the night too, only waking when the sun came
up over the bare branches of the plane trees in the street.

Aunt Maud was already at the breakfast table, her face grim and pale, when Lucilla came down with her bag and peered round the door into the dining room.

"Well?" Aunt Maud asked, without even wishing Lucilla good morning.

"What conclusion have you come to? Have you decided to be sensible or are you going to persist in your refusal of Mr. Jackson's generous proposal."

Lucilla put her bag down in the hall and came into the dining room.

Somehow just reading Nanny's words and knowing that she would be able to see the old lady very soon had given her new strength and courage.

And she found she now knew instinctively exactly how to deal with Aunt Maud.

"Thank you for your concern, Aunt," she said very politely. "I am not going to be rushed into making a hasty decision, as I believe that would be wrong. I am honoured by Mr. Jackson's proposal, but I need a little time to think about it as everything has happened to me so quickly and it has quite taken me by surprise."

Before her aunt could comment, Lucilla carried on speaking,

"I appreciate, Aunt, that you don't wish to have me living under the same roof as yourself at the present time and I don't wish to cause any inconvenience to you while you are preparing for your wedding, so I am going to stay in the country for a while – "

"Where? What do you mean by this?" her aunt demanded. "You cannot just go gadding off at will. If you wish to marry a decent gentleman such as Mr. Jackson, you must behave in a respectable manner!"

Lucilla smiled.

"I shall be perfectly respectable, aunt. I am going to stay with an old family friend in a very quiet village in Hampshire."

Aunt Maud seemed at a loss for words and Lucilla took advantage of her silence to ask if she might sit down and eat some porridge before she left, as she was extremely hungry, having eaten nothing since yesterday's breakfast and the smell of the porridge, which normally she did not like at all, was making her stomach rumble.

"I suppose so," Aunt Maud muttered, frowning at her. "But, Lucilla, I hope that you are not thinking about running off with the fine clothes I have purchased for you since you came here. I have spent a considerable amount of money on your wardrobe in the happy anticipation that you would make a good match – and I shall be very angry if I do not see some kind of return for that expense."

Lucilla poured milk over her porridge and added a sprinkle of sugar.

Suddenly she did not care if her aunt disapproved of her or not.

"Please don't worry, Aunt," she said, "I will take away only what I came with."

"And what explanation am I then to give to Lady Armstrong and Ethel for your sudden disappearance?"

"Please tell them exactly what I have just told you," Lucilla replied, as she finished her porridge. "That I am going away to think over Mr. Jackson's proposal."

She got up from the table and went out into the hall, saying 'goodbye' over her shoulder to her aunt, who stayed sitting in silence and did not offer her any good wishes.

"Hoskins, would you bring my coat?" Lucilla asked the housekeeper, who was just about to clear the table.

Hoskins stared at Lucilla's face and for a moment she wondered if by chance the woman could see the mark on her cheek where Aunt Maud had slapped her.

"It's very cold outside today, my Lady," Hoskins said. "Your old velvet won't keep the chill out at all. Why don't you wear that lovely pink coat? The new one? I can tell by that big bag you're carrying you be going off on a journey."

"Oh – no, I couldn't." Lucilla mumbled.

She did not like to think of the fact that Ethel had only bought it for her because she was then hoping that Harkness Jackson might propose and she wanted Lucilla to look pretty for him.

'Ethel doesn't really care about me one bit,' she said to herself again. 'She just wants me to accept Mr. Jackson's proposal so that she will not be the only girl in London marrying a rich old American and maybe so that she will not feel so lonely after she's married Mortimer.'

But then Lucilla remembered how lovely the coat felt when she wore it and how warm and comforting it was.

And she recalled that thick bundle of money that Ethel had taken out of her handbag and how it had seemed just as thick, even after she had paid for the coat.

'Ethel could buy a hundred coats like that one if she wanted to,' she reflected. 'She probably has forgotten that she gave it to me already.'

And so she smiled at Hoskins,

"You are right, Hoskins. I will take the new coat. It's in my bedroom."

The housekeeper's thin face broke into a smile, as she rushed up the stairs to fetch it.

"Take good care of yourself, my Lady," she said in a low voice, when she returned and was helping Lucilla into the coat.

"I shall miss you."

Lucilla's heart suddenly seemed full, as she stepped out into the frosty sunshine of the winter morning.

'So there are a few good kind people in the world after all!' she thought. 'I never knew that Hoskins cared about me.'

And she set off at a brisk pace for the Train Station, fingering Nanny Grove's note in her pocket, feeling both hopeful and nervous as she embarked on her journey to Hampshire.

CHAPTER FIVE

Lucilla peered out of the window of the train at the countryside flashing past.

She was glad that she was wearing the pink coat, as it really was a very cold day, even though the sun shone down brightly over the wintry fields and the clustered buildings of farms and villages.

There were many stops along the way, but at last the train pulled into Appleton, which Lucilla had been told was the stop for the village of Ferndean.

Lucilla jumped off the train and looked around for someone to help her.

A small man with a large moustache came out of the Ticket Office and touched his cap.

"Appleton Hall, is it, miss?" he enquired in a warm accent that reminded her of the voices of the Dorset people, who lived round her old home.

"Are they meeting you with the carriage?"

Lucilla shook her head.

She had never heard of Appleton Hall, although it sounded impressive.

"I am going to Ferndean. Is it very far from here?"

The man looked surprised and Lucilla realised that he was staring at her glorious pink coat and so he must be thinking that she was someone important and special.

"Pardon me, miss. But I took you for one of the Marquis's visitors from the look of you," the man was now saying. "But Ferndean is just a stone's throw from The Hall, miss. Shall I send for a pony and trap?"

Lucilla looked up at the bright blue winter sky and the sunlight gleaming off the roofs of the houses and shops in the centre of Appleton.

"If it isn't very far, I think I should like to walk."

"Then you must go through the Market Square and down the hill and over the bridge and, if you keep a good pace, miss, you will be at Ferndean village in less than half an hour," the man told her.

Lucilla thanked him and set off, thankful that her bag held only a few of her old clothes and was not very heavy.

She crossed the bridge over the river, as the man had told her and then the road led out into the countryside through fields of sheep and cows.

'Whoever owns this land is a good farmer,' she thought, noticing the neatly trimmed hedges and the well-fed contented animals.

Ferndean village lay in a wooded valley with a little stream winding through it.

There were not many cottages and all of them had brightly painted front doors and thatched roofs.

There was no one about to ask where Holly Cottage might be, but, as Lucilla looked around, she noticed that the smallest cottage on the banks of the stream had a little holly tree covered in red berries in the front garden.

Its windows were full of the bright geraniums that Nanny had always kept on the nursery windowsills when Lucilla was a child.

Lucilla tapped on the green-painted front door and then waited, but no one came.

'Perhaps I am wrong and this isn't Holly Cottage after all,' she wondered.

And then, for one terrible moment, she wondered if it might be that she had come to the right place, but that Nanny Groves had died and her journey had been in vain.

Then she heard a rustling from inside the door and a voice called out,

"Who is there?"

"Nanny! It's me, Lucilla!"

Slowly the green door opened and a very tiny old woman peered up at Lucilla.

"My dear! Well – *what* a surprise! Come in, come in!"

"Nanny!" Lucilla cried and bent down to hug the old lady.

She was shocked to see how much older Nanny Groves looked. She seemed to have shrunk in the years since she had left Wellsprings Place to retire to Hampshire.

But Nanny Groves's little blue eyes were as bright as ever and her white hair was tied in the same neat bun that Lucilla remembered so well from her nursery days.

"You must go before me, my dear," Nanny Groves said, when at last Lucilla released her from the hug. "I am very slow these days. Go on into the parlour and put your bag down."

The parlour was warm from a fire that crackled in the grate and the sunlight that filtered in through the red and pink geraniums on the windowsill shed a bright glow over the room.

"Only you could make those geraniums flower in the winter!" Lucilla cried, as Nanny followed her slowly into the room.

Nanny smiled, her face as wrinkled as a walnut.

"Hang that beautiful coat, my dear, behind the door – you can see where. There is tea already in the pot and we shall sit down and rest awhile and enjoy it."

Lucilla could see that even the short walk to the door had been difficult for the old lady and she helped her to a chair and then poured out the tea before she sat down herself.

"You are looking so well, my dear," Nanny Groves said. "You have often been in my thoughts, as I was very worried for you after your terrible loss, but – you have a fine colour in your cheeks."

Lucilla laughed and then explained that she had just walked from the Station and that it must be the cold air that was making her look so fresh and well.

"Ah, but what about that coat, my dear?" Nanny asked with a twinkle in her eye. "It looks very expensive. Someone surely has been spoiling you? I wouldn't have thought it of your Aunt Maud, but perhaps I am wrong – "

Lucilla was just taking a sip of tea, when suddenly she found that it was catching in her throat.

She did not want to think of Aunt Maud, who had been so cruel to her over the last months – or, indeed of Ethel, who had only bought that coat for her because she wanted her to accept Harkness Jackson's proposal.

"But, Nanny, how are you?" she asked, swallowing her tea. "I feel so bad that I have not seen you for such a long time and I did not even reply to your kind letter."

Nanny Groves shook her head.

"You must not trouble yourself, dear Lucilla. I did not expect to hear from you, as I knew that you must have been out of your mind with grief."

Lucilla nodded, not trusting herself to speak, but she could tell by the caring look in Nanny Groves's blue eyes that she understood exactly how Lucilla felt when she remembered the loss of her dear Mama and Papa.

"And how is your aunt?" the old lady asked after a moment.

"She is well and she will be getting married very soon to a Mr. Pargetter."

Nanny Groves blinked in surprise.

"Goodness me, my dear! That is the last thing I was expecting you to tell me. I rather thought it was you who had become engaged and that was the reason for your visit to me here."

Lucilla shook her head.

"No, Nanny, I am not engaged."

"And why not, Lucilla? Such a pretty girl as you should have had lots and lots of proposals by now from all the handsome young gentlemen in London. Was there no one you liked?"

Lucilla sighed deeply and explained to Nanny about Harkness Jackson's proposal.

"I think Aunt Maud would really like me to marry him, but I – he is much much older than me and he is an American – "

Nanny Groves laughed.

"Neither of those things should matter the tiniest bit, if you loved him."

"I don't!" Lucilla asserted. "I really don't, Nanny."

"Then you must not marry him," Nanny said in the determined voice that Lucilla remembered so well from her childhood.

"But I don't know what else to do, Nanny. I told Aunt Maud that I would think about it and she does not want me to stay with her any more, unless I accept Mr. Jackson's offer."

"Do you feel safe and happy when you are with this man?" the old woman asked in the same determined tone.

"He is very rich and he does seem to care for me," Lucilla replied.

Nanny did not look as if she believed Lucilla.

"Will you like to be still with him when he is an old man and you are older too?"

Lucilla shook her head, wishing that Nanny Groves would be quiet, but she was still talking on.

"And, most importantly, my dear, do you want to have his children?"

"No!" Lucilla cried in horror. "I cannot imagine anything more appalling!"

"Then you cannot possibly be his wife. Finding the right person to spend your life with is the most important thing you will ever do. For, if you make the wrong choice, you will be unhappy for the rest of your days."

"Oh, Nanny! I know! I know!" Lucilla cried, her eyes filling up. "I feel that so strongly."

"There must be someone you like – " Nanny said in a lighter tone, a glint of mischief in her bright blue eyes.

Lucilla felt a little shiver run down her spine as she remembered the dark-eyed young man at Ethel's party.

"I did meet – someone," she murmured, "but – "

Nanny Groves smiled.

"I can tell by the look on your face how much you like him, whoever he is,"

"But he did not seem to – like me very much – "

Nanny Groves shrugged her bent shoulders.

"If he is yours, my dear, you will find him again. And if not, someone else will come to you. And in the meantime you must treat Holly Cottage as your home."

Lucilla sighed, as she felt herself relaxing for the first time in a very long while.

Somehow she had always felt cold in Aunt Maud's unfriendly house and constantly afraid she might be told off or criticised.

Nanny Groves's little parlour was deliciously warm and the armchair she sat in was soft and comfortable.

"My dear Lucilla, your eyes are closing!" Nanny pointed out. "Why don't you now take yourself up to the spare bedroom and you can rest properly."

Lucilla shook herself, blinking in the flickering firelight.

"I don't want to be rude, Nanny!"

"Nonsense. You are absolutely worn out. I shall not take offence at all, Lucilla, if you go upstairs and take a nap! It's so good to have you here with me, my dear!"

Lucilla made her way up the steep wooden stairs to the tiny bedroom under the eaves. She had never been in such a small room before, but everything she needed was there.

A little bed with its white quilted cover and a deep feather mattress, a small wardrobe for her clothes and a washstand with a flowered jug and bowl and a pretty heart-shaped mirror.

*

As soon as her head touched the soft pillow, Lucilla was fast asleep and she did not wake up until the bright rays of winter sunshine came streaming through the small window the next morning.

"Nanny, I'm really sorry!" she cried, as she hurried downstairs and into the parlour. "I've slept and slept!"

"Indeed you have," the old lady said with a smile, as she sat knitting in her chair by the fire. "You've missed dinner and breakfast as well! In fact, it's almost time for luncheon."

Lucilla felt embarrassed.

"Can I help you with luncheon, Nanny?" she asked. "I am not much of a cook, but I could help you to prepare the vegetables."

Nanny Groves laughed.

"No need for that, my dear. All my meals are sent down from Appleton Hall.

"Don't look so surprised, my dear!" she continued, seeing the expression on Lucilla's face. "Do you remember me telling you stories about a little boy called Dermot?"

"Yes, I think so. He lived in a big house and used to ride a white pony. And didn't you look after him before you came to help my Mama and Papa take care of me?"

"That's right! Well, then – little Dermot is now a Marquis and lives at Appleton Hall. And he makes sure that I have everything I need."

Nanny Groves looked very happy as she said this.

Then she added,

"But I am always ready for a cup of tea. Why don't you go and make one for us? You might even find some freshly baked bread and strawberry jam in the kitchen!"

Lucilla was not at all surprised to find that Nanny's tiny kitchen was absolutely spotless and that everything from the snowy white apron on the back of the door to the big brown teapot on the dresser was neatly arranged in its proper place.

She put on Nanny's apron, tying the strings at her waist and she had just found the china jar that held the tea leaves, when there was a knock at the front door.

"I'll get it!" she called, remembering how long it had taken Nanny to answer the door yesterday.

But, as Lucilla stepped into the hall, the front door was already opening and a huge bunch of pink roses was pushed through it, followed by a tall young man.

He stared at Lucilla over the mass of pink blooms.

"Who on earth are you?" he asked in surprise, a frown creasing his dark brows.

It was *him*!

The young man with dark hair who had haunted Lucilla's thoughts ever since Ethel's engagement party.

Her heart leapt inside her, hammering against her chest and she so wanted to cry out to him '*it's me, don't you remember?*'

But, as his brown eyes gazed into hers, she realised that he did not recognise her.

He had no idea that they had once met and spoken to each other.

"I am just making some tea – " she replied, when at last she could force her voice to speak.

The young man looked puzzled, but after a moment he smiled at her.

"Good idea. I would like one very much indeed, if you don't mind. Just the right thing on a cold morning like this."

He strode towards the parlour and, as he passed, the bouquet of roses brushed against the white apron Lucilla was wearing.

'He takes me for a servant,' she thought, looking down at the teapot she was holding.

Her heart was still beating so fast that she felt quite shaky.

Whatever was he doing, here in Nanny Groves's little cottage?

With a great effort, she pulled herself together and went back into the kitchen.

She found a large tray and put plates, cups, saucers and a milk jug, sugar bowl and slop basin on it, struggling to control her trembling hands as she laid everything out.

Then in a panic she looked around for the kettle. It was nowhere to be seen. Of course not, for it would be simmering over the fire in the parlour, where it had been yesterday.

'I can't go in there,' she whispered to herself. 'I just can't see him again, it's too much. But I've got to – '

She picked up the heavy tray and stood dithering for a moment, trying to pluck up her courage until she heard footsteps in the hall.

The kitchen door opened a crack.

He had returned.

"Nanny says, whatever you do, please don't forget the strawberry jam," he pronounced, peering at her with a mischievous expression.

"Oh!" Lucilla jumped nervously – and the cups and saucers rattled on the tray.

"Shall I take that for you?"

He came into the kitchen and picked up the tray.

"I can tell that this isn't your normal occupation. I thought for a short moment, when I saw you just then, that Nanny had found herself a parlour maid! But she has put me right."

"Thank you so much," Lucilla said, keeping her voice as steady as she could. "I – will now try and find the jam – "

"It's in that blue and white pot on the dresser," he volunteered and then, as he saw how she could not help staring at him, he smiled and gave a tiny wink.

"And – the bread is in the big brown crock over there!"

And then he was gone, expertly manhandling the heavy tray through the kitchen door.

Lucilla took a deep breath.

He seemed so different, suddenly. So cheerful and light-hearted and friendly.

But he still seemed to have no idea that they had ever met before.

She found a big crusty loaf of brown bread in the crock he had indicated and cut thin slices from it, spreading them with butter and the luscious red strawberry jam from the blue and white pot.

Then she laid them all out on a big china plate and carried them through to the parlour.

"Thank you for doing all this, my dear!" Nanny Groves said. "I find making tea irksome and boring at my age, but I do so love to drink it. Would you pour it out for us, Lucilla? The tea is all ready brewing in the pot and Dermot has kindly added water to the leaves."

The young man was now sitting in a most relaxed manner on the sofa with his arms along the back of it and his legs stretched out to the fire, as if he felt completely at home in Nanny's little parlour.

"Did you know that we both have something in common," he said, as Lucilla passed him a cup and saucer.

Her face was warm with shyness and she wondered what he might mean.

Had he remembered that they both knew Ethel?

"Would you care for some bread and jam?" she asked him, turning away so that he could not see that she was flustered.

"I rather think we should ask Nanny!" he said with

a laugh. "What do you think, Nanny? Have I been well behaved? Or is it plain bread and butter for me, today?"

Nanny clucked her tongue and shook her head.

"Well, I don't know what to say, Dermot. It was most impolite of you to mistake my house guest for the parlour maid!"

The young man leapt to his feet and, standing in front of Lucilla, made a deep bow.

"Lady Lucilla Welton, I believe," he said in a low courteous voice. "Please will you accept the most humble and sincere apologies of the Marquis of Castlebury for his foolish and insensitive behaviour just now."

Lucilla gave a little gasp of surprise.

"Can you forgive me?" he asked, his brown eyes glinting with merriment, "for I am not sure I can stomach bread and butter all on its own!"

"Dermot!" Nanny added sternly. "You must allow Lucilla time to make up her mind to forgive you and not push her. I wonder if you have remembered any of the manners I tried to teach you in the nursery."

"Oh, please, don't worry," Lucilla cried. "I came to answer the door in an apron and so it would be perfectly natural to mistake me for a parlour maid – if you had never met me before – "

She looked up at him, watching his face for any sign of acknowledgement that he might have remembered Ethel's party.

But he was smiling at her in a cheerful and relaxed way.

"There – you see, Nanny! Lucilla forgives me, as she understands exactly what happened. All I noticed was the apron, as I was looking at her from behind the bunch of roses I had brought for my favourite lady."

Nanny was still looking stern.

"Don't you think you can get around me like that, young Dermot. What do you say, Lucilla? Shall we allow this young gentleman some jam with his bread?"

Lucilla smiled to herself, as she remembered how strict Nanny had always been about good manners.

"Of course," she agreed, "I know how hard it is to be deprived of jam. It happened to me many times when I forgot my P's and Q's!"

The Marquis of Castlebury sat down again on the sofa.

"Dear Nanny. What a tyrant she was. But how I missed her when I went away to school and she deserted us to go and look after you, Lucilla!"

"You must be happy to have her living so close to you now," Lucilla remarked, as she passed him the plate of bread and jam.

"We are very lucky, my sister and I, that she agreed to come and be with us," the Marquis added, as he helped himself to a large slice, "as her strawberry jam is surely the best in the world!"

Nanny shook her head again.

"Flattery!" she sighed. "It'll get you nowhere. I am now going to put my roses in some water before they wilt in the heat of the fire and I shall expect you two to behave politely and respectfully to each other while I'm out of the room!"

The old lady climbed awkwardly to her feet and gathered up the large bunch of flowers.

"They are very beautiful," Lucilla said, as Nanny went slowly out of the parlour, her arms full of roses.

"The best our hothouses have to offer," the Marquis replied, finishing his bread and jam. "I have to go away for a while and I will miss Nanny very much indeed. She is my favourite person in the world, next to my sister Violet."

Lucilla nodded.

"And mine, too, since Mama and Papa died."

"Oh, I am so sorry. How awful. Are you all on your own – or do you have brothers and sisters?"

"It is just myself," Lucilla told him, willing herself not to cry.

The Marquis's brown eyes then turned dark with concern.

"So, where do you live? At your parents' home? Where is that?"

"I – am staying here for a while. My family home is up for sale, as there is not enough money to run it now that Papa is gone."

The Marquis shook his head sadly.

"I do sympathise. The upkeep of an estate can be a huge burden, if it is properly run. Some of the local gentry seem happy to send their servants and farm workers away when they are no longer able to earn their keep, but I could never do that. They have given the best of their lives to my family and it is my duty to support them in their time of need."

Lucilla recalled what Nanny had told her about her meals sent down to Holly Cottage from Appleton Hall.

"I agree with you!" she said. "Our servants – those who had been with us at Wellsprings Place for a long time were almost like family."

"And then, of course, one has responsibilities to one's house," the Marquis was saying. "Appleton Hall has stood for centuries and I intend that it shall stand for many more – but the restoration work that I am having to do is costing me very dear."

Lucilla then thought about Wellsprings Place and all the plans her Papa had made for repairs to the roof and interior decorations, plans that would never be carried out.

"It is, indeed, a huge responsibility," she sighed.

The Marquis's eyes flashed suddenly.

"The great houses of England are one of our finest assets!" he trumpeted. "And we must do all in our power to protect them and to promote all their glories at home and abroad. That is why I am going away for a while."

Lucilla felt herself turning cold at the thought of him disappearing so soon after she had found him again.

She was about to ask him where he was going and for how long, when he spoke again.

"But, Lucilla, you must come up to The Hall before I go. Please, will you join us for luncheon tomorrow?" he asked, rising to his feet and standing in front of her.

"That is if Nanny can spare you," he added quickly, as the old lady appeared in the parlour door.

"Of course I can!" Nanny Groves said, making her way back to her seat by the fire. "Lucilla mustn't spend all her time cooped up here with me!"

"Nanny, I really don't mind a bit, I love being here with you!" Lucilla cried, but even as she said it, her heart began to beat faster at the thought of the next day.

The Marquis said his goodbyes and Lucilla watched from the parlour window as he made his way along the garden path to the little front gate.

'What is it about him that makes me feel like this?' she thought, looking at his dark hair and broad shoulders as he walked away from her.

But she could find no answer, although her heart was beating so fast that it was shaking her whole body.

CHAPTER SIX

Lucilla had always thought that Wellsprings Place, where she had grown up, was the loveliest country house she had ever seen.

But, as she walked gingerly up the curved drive to the Marquis of Castlebury's home, her breath making a little cloud in the cold air, she thought there was something about Appleton Hall that was especially beautiful.

Was it the soft colour of the honey-coloured stone? Or the graceful proportions of the tall windows? Or just the atmosphere of welcome that seemed to emanate from the elegant porch and the wide front door?

Lucilla pushed her cold hands deep into the pockets of her pink coat and stood still for a moment, looking up at the old house and trying to make up her mind just exactly why she found it so appealing.

Then she heard a shrill yapping and a small white dog raced towards her and started jumping up excitedly.

"Daisy!" a girl's voice called. "Oh dear, I am so sorry, she is going to ruin your lovely coat with her muddy paws!"

Lucilla looked down at the dog's little snub-nosed face and bulging black eyes and she laughed at its comical expression.

"It really doesn't matter! I am sure the mud will brush away."

"You are very sweet," remarked the tall dark-haired young woman who was approaching her across the wide lawn in the front of the house.

"Daisy is so naughty about jumping up, especially if she likes somebody."

She held out her hand to Lucilla.

"I am Violet Castlebury, Dermot's sister. And you must be Lucilla."

Violet's eyes were as soft and dark as pansies and Lucilla could tell from the shape of her eyebrows and her elegant nose that she was indeed the Marquis's sister.

"My brother was so very amused to meet another of Nanny Groves's charges!" Violet was saying. "We often wondered, when we were younger, about the little girl she had left us for."

The little dog was scrabbling at Lucilla's coat hem as if it would have liked to jump into her arms.

"Daisy, do get down!" Violet exclaimed, picking up her pet and kissing the top of its head. "She adores you, it's obvious! But we have been looking at the spring bulbs, which are just coming up in the Park and her paws are very muddy. You must be cold, Lucilla – do come inside."

Inside Appleton Hall was even more glorious than Lucilla had expected.

As she now stepped into the hall, she breathed in the fragrant scents of lavender wax and of the white lilies that stood in a great vase on top of the piano.

"My brother loves music," Violet went on, as she led Lucilla into the drawing room, "and he insists that the hall has the best acoustics of any room in the house, so he must have his piano there!"

Lucilla remembered how he had come to the little salon at the Armstrongs, when he had heard her playing Chopin, but she said nothing.

The Marquis had obviously forgotten that day and would not have said anything to his sister and so Violet would not know that they had met before.

As they sat by the marble fireplace in the drawing room, Violet asked how long Lucilla was planning to stay at Holly Cottage.

"I – really don't know," Lucilla replied.

She looked away from Violet and then turned to the dog that was now sitting on the sofa beside her, resting its head in her lap and gazing up at her with beseeching eyes.

Violet smiled at her.

"You must forgive me, but Daisy has taken such a fancy to you. And I am about to go away to the Continent. I wondered if – but no, I must not impose on you."

"If you were going to ask me if I would look after her for you, I should love to!" Lucilla enthused.

Daisy's snub-nosed face was very appealing and it was so comforting to feel the dog's warm little body lying against her.

"I may be away some time," Violet said, a shadow passing over her pale face.

Lucilla was wondering just how she might explain, without revealing too much of what had happened to her in London, that she would probably be staying with Nanny Groves for quite a long while, when the drawing room door swung open and the Marquis came in.

"Violet! My darling sister! You are looking utterly tragic."

He leant over the back of Violet's chair and ruffled her hair affectionately.

"Our guest will get quite the wrong impression of life at Appleton Hall."

Lucilla's heart skipped a beat, as he left Violet and came over to take her hand.

It was almost too much to have him so close to her, even more handsome than he was yesterday.

"Lady Lucilla – welcome!" he said and her skin tingled as she felt his lips brush the back of her fingers.

"So – and what have you girls been discussing?" he continued, balancing on the arm of the sofa and stretching his long legs out to the fire.

"Lucilla has most kindly offered to look after Daisy while we are abroad," Violet responded, "but – it was very wrong of me to ask her."

She turned to Lucilla,

"You must have many calls upon your time and attention and it was quite unfair of me to presume that you might look after my dog."

Almost as if she understood what was being said, Daisy gave a little whimper and climbed into Lucilla's lap.

The Marquis laughed.

"No one asked you for your opinion, Daisy! And you know she will be perfectly well cared for here, Violet, with the housekeeper and the maids to fuss over her."

"Yes, of course, I know, Dermot, but – "

"My sister hates to go away and leave her beloved creatures behind."

"I do! It is very foolish of me," Violet said and she smiled, even though the sad look still lingered in her eyes. "I even feel miserable that I won't be here to see all the daffodils I have planted come into bloom. And the birds in the aviary will be starting their nests. I can't bear to leave them."

Violet's eyes were so full of pain that Lucilla could not help but feel sorry for her.

"Please – if it makes it any easier for you, I would really love to look after Daisy and the birds – and even the daffodils!"

The Marquis raised his dark brows at Lucilla and was about to say something when the butler arrived to announce that luncheon was served.

So instead of speaking, he slid off the arm of the sofa.

"Let's go and eat!" he suggested, "and afterwards, Lady Lucilla, I would be delighted to escort you on a little tour of our estate."

The luncheon was delicious with soup and fish and a green salad of delicate leaves from the glasshouses on the Castlebury estate.

Lucilla was happy to sit back and enjoy her food, as Violet and Dermot reminisced happily on their childhood and the happy days when Nanny Groves had presided over the nursery at Appleton Hall.

As the butler brought fruit for their dessert to the table, the Marquis turned to Lucilla.

"I must apologise for Violet and myself – here we are talking nineteen to the dozen and quite ignoring you,"

"Not at all," she replied and told him how much she was enjoying their conversation, for she could tell how much they loved each other and appreciated each other's company.

"I think I have quite missed out by being an only child," she murmured.

"Oh – you are so polite!" the Marquis grinned at her. "A true product of Nanny's education. You see – I told you we had something in common."

And he gave Lucilla a slight wink, just as he had done yesterday.

Lucilla looked down at her plate, hoping that the heat that was rising in her cheeks did not show too much.

He was so different from the man she had met at the Armstrongs.

He now seemed so happy – almost flirtatious – and he did not seem to have any idea how it made her feel to see him and to be so close to him.

Now he was standing up from the table and inviting her to walk with him.

"Let's leave Violet and Daisy to doze in front of the fire," he suggested, as the butler brought their coats.

As they stepped out of the front door, the Marquis eyed the cut of Lucilla's coat with approval and suddenly she wished she had her old velvet coat with her instead.

'I know that this coat makes me look good,' she thought, 'but I cannot bear to remember who bought it for me and why!'

Outside the sun was beginning to break through the mist and long rays of light lit up the broad avenues of trees and the expanses of lawn surrounding Appleton Hall.

"I am rather worried about my sister," the Marquis confided, as soon as they left the house and headed toward the Park. "She is becoming like an old woman, always wanting to stay at home and fuss with her dogs and birds."

Lucilla did not really know what to say to this, but she pointed out that it was natural for any woman who was kind-hearted to care for the well-being of her pets.

"Yes!" he agreed, "but she should get married and have a family! I should miss her, of course, but – "

"Perhaps she has not met anyone she likes," Lucilla commented, not quite daring to look at him.

The Marquis sighed.

"Oh, she has, that is the trouble. She was engaged to be married, but, alas, her fiancé was killed, fighting in the Boer War. And now she will not look at anyone else."

"Did she really love him?" Lucilla asked, trying to ignore the tight feeling building in her chest. "If she did, then perhaps – she just cannot – love someone else – "

"It was a long time ago."

"Even so, it would not be right for her to try and – love someone she did not really care for."

The Marquis was striding along quickly now, his feet leaving wet prints as he trod across the damp grass.

Suddenly he turned round to face Lucilla.

"You speak with conviction," he said, looking into her eyes, "almost with passion. I think you must be talking from some kind of personal experience."

Lucilla's face was so hot she had to put her hands up to her cheeks so the smooth leather of her gloves might cool them.

"I am sorry," the Marquis looked away from her. "It is really unfair of me to speculate about your personal and private affairs in this way."

"No, it's just that – I am in a difficult position."

Lucilla was longing to tell him everything, all about Harkness Jackson, although she knew that it would not be right to speak about this with someone who was a relative stranger and – a gentleman.

But she did not want to close the conversation.

"I – have had a proposal of marriage," she stuttered, "and – I cannot accept it, because I do not – could not – love the gentleman concerned. And so, perhaps I can feel some sympathy with your sister – "

The Marquis's dark brows were creased in a frown.

"I am sorry to hear that you are in this situation," he said. "But Violet is older than you are – she *must* marry soon."

"Have you ever been in love, my Lord?"

As soon as the words were out of Lucilla's mouth, she wished she had not said them, for the lines on the Marquis's face deepened.

"Yes!"

He almost spat the word out.

And he began to walk faster again, so that Lucilla had to trot to keep up with him.

"And – would you – " she asked him breathlessly, thinking that now she had begun, she might as well carry on, for she very much wanted him to understand what she was trying to tell him, "have married that person, the one you loved?"

"I asked her to marry me! She led me to believe that she would be my wife – and then – "

His hands clenched into tight fists as he spoke,

"She turned her back on me, for the sake of another man's greater fortune."

Lucilla stumbled over a patch of rough grass and almost fell to her knees.

He was talking about Ethel!

It could only be her he was referring to.

"Lucilla!"

The Marquis turned back, reaching out for her arm to steady her.

"Are you all right? I am being quite thoughtless, rushing ahead like this."

"No, it is I who is thoughtless," Lucilla answered, when she caught her breath. "We should not be talking about a subject that is so painful to you."

"Oh, please don't concern yourself. I don't care who knows it," the Marquis said, his eyes glinting with a bitter light. "She has betrayed me for a man I swear she does not love. But – enough of that. Let's turn back. The grass is still damp, even though the sun is out and your shoes will be soaked."

Lucilla had not noticed that the ground underfoot was soggy and that the water was staining her shoes.

"I am sure that you will recover in time," she said, as the Marquis was still looking morose.

He shook his head.

"I cannot believe that I will ever care for a woman again."

"Then – can you not see how your sister must feel? If she has lost her one true love?"

"It's not the same. Her fiancé died. He did not say he loved her, promise to marry her and then betray her."

His eyes were dark and unreadable as he looked at her and Lucilla knew that she should say no more.

Then he smiled at her, although his eyes remained guarded.

"Dear Lucilla – you are a kind soul. And there is so much more of the estate to see. Come, I shall take you to the aviary."

They turned back towards the house and he led her to a stunning construction of metal and wire with domes and vaults to rival the great Crystal Palace, although on a far smaller scale.

There were trees planted inside it and all over the branches wooden nest boxes with holes for doors and neat little roofs were hanging.

Lucilla gasped in sheer delight as she watched the brightly coloured birds flitting from twig to twig, flicking their wings at each other and inspecting the boxes.

"They know better how to live their lives than we humans," the Marquis remarked gloomily, as he stood by her side.

For a moment she wondered what he meant.

And then she realised that the bright birds were all in pairs. Some sat side by side in the trees, their feathers fluffed up against the cold. Others were peeping out from the cosy nest boxes.

Look as she might, all through the huge aviary, she could not see a single bird on its own.

'Will I ever find someone who really loves me and always wants to be by my side?' Lucilla thought and she shivered as she pictured herself alone and forever fleeing the unwanted attentions of the likes of Harkness Jackson.

The Marquis seemed lost in sadness now, his eyes turned inward to his own painful thoughts.

'He is so changeable,' Lucilla mused. 'He is like a stormy spring day, one moment bright and full of sunshine and the next as perturbed and miserable as can be.'

Her heart turned over in her chest as she looked at him, at his dark hair and his strong brooding face.

She wanted to reach out to him, touch his arm and try to comfort him, but she did not dare.

"You are cold!" the Marquis queried. "I have kept you outside for far too long. Let's go back to the fire."

As they walked along the terrace that ran in front of the house, he apologised to her for talking so much about himself.

"It's all foolish nonsense," he said. "And I should not burden you with it. It was most rude of me."

"It is causing you great pain, my Lord, and surely it is good to talk about issues that are troubling us, for then they become smaller in our minds."

He smiled at her, his dark mood evaporating.

"You sound just like Nanny!"

Lucilla felt her own heart lightening too.

"I'm sure it is a good thing you are going away," she said. "To be abroad will distract and entertain you – "

"Yes," the Marquis replied with a bitter little smile "and there will be many miles – and the English Channel – between Ethel and myself."

He did not seem to notice that he had spoken her name out loud, but Lucilla felt her skin suddenly recoiling from the fur at her wrists.

If he knew that Ethel had bought the coat for her, just what would he say?

He would be disgusted.

He must never, never find out.

"Oh, Lucilla – you must stay for tea!" Violet cried, coming down to meet them in the hall.

The butler was approaching to take Lucilla's coat and hang it up, but she stopped him.

She had to get away and take the coat that she now found completely hateful with her.

"You are very kind, but I must get back to Holly Cottage and look after Nanny. She finds making her own tea a chore now – "

Violet reached out and put her arms around Lucilla, kissing her on the cheek.

"It has been so lovely to meet you, Lucilla. You are welcome here any time you would like to come and visit us. I am sure Dermot will be just as happy as I am to see you again."

The Marquis nodded.

"Absolutely," he said and then a mischievous look crept into his eyes. "And as for Daisy – she will be quite bereft without you!"

Lucilla bent down to pat the little dog, which was fussing around her feet.

"I really would be very happy to look after her for you while you are away," she confirmed. "It would be no trouble for me at all."

Violet gazed at her, her soft brown eyes full of tears.

"Oh Lucilla, you are so kind. She really does seem to have taken to you. And I have too! I never had a sister, but – if I had, I would have liked her to be just like you!"

The two girls embraced and Lucilla hurried away down the drive, anxious to be back at Holly Cottage before the afternoon light began to fall into dusk.

As she laid the tea tray in Nanny's little kitchen, the Marquis's face was there constantly before her eyes, as she remembered everything he had said and all the shades of emotion and passion that had passed through him.

'I have never in my life met anyone quite like him,' she thought to herself. 'He feels everything so deeply.'

And, try as she might, she could not put him out of her mind or still the feelings in her heart that seemed to grow stronger each time she thought of him.

*

"How did you like Appleton Hall?" Nanny Groves asked her, as they sipped their tea.

"Oh, it is so beautiful! Such a fine old house," and then Lucilla continued,

"Nanny – I must ask you something."

"What is it, my dear?"

"I have something that was – a gift from someone I – don't like very much."

Nanny Groves looked sharply at Lucilla.

"Have you accepted a gift from this man you spoke about yesterday?"

"No! Of course not, Nanny! But – it is difficult."

Without mentioning her name, she explained about Ethel and how she had bought the glorious pink coat and given it to Lucilla against her will.

"I think this girl wanted me to accept Mr. Jackson's proposal. She wanted me to have the coat so that I would impress him – "

"But why, my dear?"

"She herself is engaged to a friend of Mr. Jackson's – another American."

"Ah!" Nanny nodded her head. "I see. It's a bold step for a well-bred English girl to take, to marry someone so very different from her own kind. She must have hoped that she would not be the only one to make such a choice."

"Then what should I do, Nanny? The pink coat is so beautiful, yet I don't feel comfortable wearing it."

"Then you must return it, at once." Nanny replied. "Go and find one of the big baskets in the scullery – the ones that my laundry comes back in from Appleton Hall. We'll pack the coat in it and send it by rail tomorrow."

"I don't want her to know where I am," she said, suddenly feeling afraid. "They will come after me, I am sure."

"Just tell the Stationmaster not to put any return address on the basket. No one will ever be able to find out where it has come from."

Lucilla went to unhook the coat from where it was hanging in the hall. It was still a little damp from her walk back from Appleton Hall.

'I will not have a warm coat now,' she reflected, as she stroked the fur cuffs.

But, deep inside, she knew that she had made the right decision as she folded it up and carried it through into the scullery to pack it away.

She must leave her old life far behind and move on, whatever the future might hold.

*

The next morning dawned bright and sunny.

Lucilla loaded the basket into the wheelbarrow and trundled it down to the Station with one of Nanny's thick woollen shawls wrapped around her shoulders to keep her warm.

The kindly man with the big moustache came out from the Ticket Office to take it from her.

"No return address, miss? Are you sure?" he asked.

"Quite sure."

Inside the basket she had placed a note for Ethel, thanking her and saying that she did not need the pink coat anymore and wished to return it.

The Stationmaster looked rather puzzled, but took the basket from her with no further questions.

As he did so, Lucilla heard a clatter of hooves on the road behind her and a man's voice called out,

"Halloa there!"

It was the Marquis.

He came trotting up to her on a tall grey horse.

"Whatever are you doing?" he asked her, frowning down at her. "Surely you are not leaving us already?"

"Oh – no!"

"But what's that great basket? I thought it must be your luggage."

Lucilla did not know what to say.

She did not want him to know that the large basket contained her pink coat, as then she would have to think of something less that truthful to tell him about it.

Luckily he was now staring at Nanny's shawl.

"And what *are* you wearing?" he asked. "I didn't recognise you, as I rode down the street just now."

Once again, Lucilla was at a loss for words.

But now the Marquis was smiling at her.

"If I had not ridden up to see what was going on, I might have taken you for a washerwoman!"

Once again, Lucilla thought how swiftly his moods changed.

Now he seemed full of laughter and high spirits.

He leant down from the saddle, his eyes glowing with excitement.

"I am so glad I caught up with you," he whispered. "For I have had a wonderful idea. I think – I hope – that you are going to like it very much!"

Her heart beating painfully fast, Lucilla looked up at him, wondering what on earth he was about to say.

CHAPTER SEVEN

The Marquis swung himself out of the saddle and leapt down so that he was standing close to Lucilla.

He took her hand and, gazing into her eyes, he then almost exploded,

"Come to Paris with me!"

Lucilla was shocked to the core by his words.

Her heart beat fast, swelling with joy and her head was spinning with excitement.

He gripped her fingers tightly, bringing her back to earth.

"Don't you think that will be the most wonderful fun?" he asked, his brown eyes glowing.

"Yes!" Lucilla managed to whisper, as she could scarcely breathe for the tide of emotion that surged in her breast.

He wanted her to go away with him!

"It came to me yesterday – when you were leaving. It was something Violet said about wishing that you were her sister."

Lucilla wondered why he was talking about Violet.

She felt a little sad, as she realised that the Marquis was no longer gazing into her eyes.

He was looking beyond her, his face alight with fun almost as if he was already surveying the busy boulevards of Paris.

"Violet?" she asked, hoping that he would explain himself.

"Yes!" he cried. "It came to me as I watched you two together. You are so much alike with your brown hair and your slim figures."

Lucilla was thoroughly puzzled, but the Marquis was still talking.

"And when Violet spoke of you being the sister she has always longed for – why – then the idea struck me!"

"Whatever do you mean?" Lucilla drew her hand away from his, as she was feeling more confused by the moment.

"Don't you see?" the Marquis continued. "Violet is so longing to stay at home. She says she will accompany me, but I just know she will be miserable. Why don't *you* come, Lucilla? And *pretend* to be my sister? Don't you think that would be the most marvellous fun?"

"I – don't know!" Lucilla stammered.

It was hard to resist him when he stood in front of her smiling, his brown eyes so earnest and beseeching.

She did not know what to think of his proposition. It would be great fun, *yes*, to go to Paris with him.

But how would she feel if she had always to play the role of a sister? Would she be able to conceal the fact that being close to him would make her heart race with such intense and most un-sisterly emotions?

"What do you say?" he was asking now, looking anxiously at her.

"*Yes!*"

Lucilla could not help but say it, for the smile was fading from his lips and she could not bear to see him sad again.

"*I will come.*"

As soon as the words were out, she knew that she had made the right decision.

His face lit up with delight again.

"We must tell Nanny!" he suggested. "Come, I will walk back to Holly Cottage with you."

He looped the reins of his grey horse over his arm and they strolled up the road and over the bridge through bright winter sunshine, listening to small birds cheeping in the trees.

For a while they walked together without speaking and Lucilla thought that just to be with him, so quietly and companionably, was one of the most wonderful feelings she had ever experienced.

'There is something so alive about him,' she said to herself. 'He makes everything seem more beautiful and more exciting.'

Almost as if he could now read her thoughts, the Marquis turned to her, his face alight with enthusiasm.

"Spring is coming," he sighed. "You will just love Paris. It is quite perfect in the springtime."

Lucilla nodded.

She had been to Paris with Mama and Papa, but not in the spring.

And then they were at Holly Cottage.

The Marquis tied his horse to the gatepost and came inside with Lucilla.

Nanny Groves did not look pleased when she heard the Marquis's plan.

"Whatever are you thinking about, Dermot!" she exclaimed.

"Don't you think it's the best idea ever?" he said, a little anxiously, as Nanny was looking fiercely at him.

"I most certainly do not!" the old lady responded, her chin held at a very determined angle. "You are asking Lucilla to pretend to be Violet! That is not only deceitful, but is placing Lucilla in a most compromising position."

All the joy and excitement that had filled her heart only a few moments ago now evaporated like mist, as she listened to these words.

"What will you do if you meet someone in France who knows Violet? You are asking Lucilla to live a lie. And to accompany you on your journey to Paris without a chaperone would be disastrous for her reputation."

"But Nanny – Lucilla is longing to go! Look at her, she has gone quite white with disappointment."

Nanny shook her head.

"However she may feel about it, Dermot, does not alter the facts as I have just explained them to you."

"Well – " the Marquis's dark brows drew together thoughtfully. "How about if Lucilla became – my younger sister – what shall we call her? Letitia? The sister that no one has ever met, because she has always stayed at home?"

He then grinned at Nanny, his head on one side and Lucilla suddenly saw the little boy he had once been.

Nanny shook her head again.

"Dermot, you are very naughty! I suppose it's very slightly worse to have Lucilla impersonate someone you have invented."

"Absolutely!" he cried. "Of course it would have been awful, if we really met someone in France who knew Violet, but – if Lucilla is 'Letitia' – what's the problem?"

Lucilla was starting to feel a little faint, for the two of them were talking about her as if she was not there and she no longer knew if she wanted to go to Paris after all.

Nanny turned to her.

"What do you think, my dear? Do you want to go along with this madcap scheme?"

"I – don't know," Lucilla replied, and then she saw the disappointment in the Marquis's eyes, and thought of how hard it would be not to see him through all the long weeks he would be away.

Even if she had to pretend that he was her brother, at least she would be by his side and then she found herself saying,

"But – I think I – should *love* to go to Paris!"

For yes, that was the truth. The thought of being left behind and of not seeing the Marquis for week upon week, turned her heart as cold as a lump of ice.

Nanny sighed,

"Then there is nothing for it. *I* shall have to come with you."

Lucilla caught her breath in horror.

"No! Nanny Groves! You must not! It will be far too much for you!"

She thought of how slowly the old lady moved and of how often she needed to refresh herself with a peaceful nap in her armchair by the fire.

The Marquis agreed.

"Lucilla is right, Nanny. We cannot tear you away from your home."

Nanny's little chin was still held high.

"I might like to see Paris before I die," she said. "I always wanted to go there when I was a young woman, but I had a living to earn and there were children to care for."

A smile flashed across the Marquis's handsome face.

"We will travel by First Class, Nanny, and we shall stay at the best hotels. Don't you think that, with extra special care, we will be able to make you feel comfortable and happy?"

Hope was spreading its wings inside Lucilla's chest like a happy little bird. Perhaps, after all, there *was* a way she could go to France with the Marquis.

"If you really would like to go, Nanny, I could take care of you," she suggested. "I would make sure that you had everything you needed and that you never had to walk too far."

Nanny Groves tutted and shook her head.

"I don't know, Lucilla. You are still asking me to go along with an untruth! I will think about it, Dermot. I should like to talk to Lucilla and hear what she has to say. Let's leave it until tomorrow and then we will give you our decision."

He looked as if he wanted to try and persuade her on the spot, but then he thought better of it.

"All right, Nanny," he agreed. "I'll leave it to you. And Lucilla, for Goodness' sake – take that dreadful shawl off. You can't go to Paris looking like a washerwoman. Where is that lovely coat you were wearing yesterday?"

Lucilla's cheeks burned as she tried desperately to think how she would reply.

But before she could open her mouth, Nanny was explaining to the Marquis that the coat had been returned to the person who gave it to Lucilla.

"Oh! I see," he intoned and gave Lucilla a quick sideways glance. "Well – I should be going. Lucilla, will you see me to the front gate?"

Lucilla opened the front door and walked with him down the garden path, praying that her face was not as red as she feared it must be.

97

"This is the man you spoke of yesterday! You are returning the coat to him because you cannot accept his proposal?" the Marquis quizzed, his dark eyebrows raised.

It would have been all too easy for Lucilla just to nod her head in agreement. But he must have noticed the confusion in her eyes, as he continued to question her,

"He must be a gentleman of good taste to buy you such a lovely garment."

"Oh – no!"

Lucilla found the words were slipping out before she had time to think what she was saying.

"He is an American – from Texas. He would never have known to buy something lovely like that – "

She thought of Harkness Jackson's loud ties and ill-fitting suits and the unfashionable shoes he wore.

"An American!"

The Marquis's face had turned suddenly bleak.

He must be thinking of Ethel and of Mortimer, her fiancé.

Lucilla felt her face growing even hotter.

"There is a mystery, here!" he declared, looking down at her. "You received a present – a wonderful coat that makes you look like a Duchess, at the very least, if not even a Princess. Who would give you such a thing, if not a man who wanted to marry you? Or perhaps you have more than one suitor?"

Lucilla shook her head.

"No, no, it was not like that at all – it was a friend – or not a friend exactly – "

"It must be a suitor!"

"No, it was a woman," Lucilla blurted out, for she could not bear him to think that there was yet another man pursuing her.

Immediately she regretted saying this and longed to escape back to the parlour and seek refuge with Nanny, as a strange look had now come over the Marquis's strong features.

"Ethel – " he said, his voice deep with pain. "It was Ethel, wasn't it, who gave you the coat? I knew there was something oddly familiar about you. We met, did we not, at the engagement party? You are – or you were – a friend of Ethel's?"

Lucilla's heart could sink no lower.

The Marquis's brown eyes no longer seemed to see her. He was staring back into the past, totally absorbed in the woman he loved so much, the one who had caused him so much pain.

"Ethel," he was muttering under his breath. "Of course. She is marrying an American and so perhaps she introduced you to this man who then proposed to you."

He sighed.

"Only she would choose such a perfect gift for you. She has such an eye for beauty. So why did you send it back?"

Lucilla recoiled from the look of despair he threw at her.

"I – cannot really – explain," she stammered.

She wanted to tell him that Ethel was not her friend and that she had not wanted to take the coat in the first place.

And she wanted to say that, when he had told her how Ethel had betrayed him, she knew that she would not be able to wear the coat any more, that she had suddenly hated it.

But her voice would not obey her and her heart knew that he would not hear her, whatever she said, for he was completely lost in the memory of the woman he had loved so much.

He gave her a swift careless bow and untied his tall grey horse, springing up onto its back.

As she watched him canter away towards Appleton Hall, Lucilla felt warm tears begin to slide down her face.

'I cannot go!' she gasped. 'I cannot do it. He still loves her! I cannot go with him, pretending to be his sister, all the while knowing that he is only thinking of Ethel!'

*

She turned to go back to Holly Cottage, wiping her face so that Nanny should not see how upset she was.

As soon as she felt calm and composed, she went into the little parlour and sat down on the sofa.

"Nanny – I don't think that I should go to Paris," she said.

The old lady looked at her in surprise.

"Well – what a change of heart!" she exclaimed.

Lucilla went on, struggling to keep her voice level,

"All the things that you said were right, Nanny. I should not go."

Nanny was silent for a few moments, her bright blue eyes searching Lucilla's face.

Lucilla hoped that the old lady could not read her thoughts, could not see how upset she was and how deeply she minded not going and not being with the Marquis.

"And Nanny, it would be very difficult for you to travel all that way."

Nanny smiled.

"Now that I have made my mind up to it, I might be very disappointed not to go!"

Lucilla now felt that whichever way she turned, she seemed to be making things worse and she leaned against the arm of the sofa with a sigh of despair, as Nanny carried on speaking.

"My dear, a moment ago, the trip to Paris was your dearest wish. I don't understand why you have changed your mind so quickly."

Lucilla looked down, trying to avoid the old lady's inquiring eyes and saw that she was still wearing Nanny's shawl.

"I have no smart clothes, Nanny!" she told her and that was certainly the truth. "Paris is the most fashionable City in Europe. I cannot go there with all my old things!"

"Ah, so that's it. I knew you had been crying when you came in just now. Has the Marquis been teasing you about your wardrobe? He really is very naughty."

"No one would ever believe that I was his sister if I turned up dressed in my old clothes with a shawl of yours draped over them!"

But Nanny was looking thoughtful.

"Perhaps you might not need to pretend to be his sister, if I was with you as your chaperone."

"No, Nanny!" Lucilla cried, her heart in her mouth. "What if someone met me who might tell my aunt and the man who wants to marry me where I was?"

"Yes, perhaps that's not such a good idea."

"No, Nanny. So – you see, I really cannot go!"

Lucilla sat back on the sofa, believing that at last the matter was settled.

Nanny sighed.

"What a shame. As I think that Dermot would have enjoyed your company very much."

Lucilla's heart turned over.

"Please, Nanny, I do think we should stop talking about this wild idea. I can't go, I have nothing to wear."

Nanny's blue eyes were twinkling now in rather a mischievous way.

"Your Mama always had such beautiful clothes. What happened to them all?"

"I think they are still at Wellsprings Place," Lucilla replied. "I expect they will all go when the house is sold. I could not take much with me when I moved in with Aunt Maud. Her house is quite small – and I was so upset, I just wanted to get away."

"Why don't you go back there and see if there isn't something you might like to wear?"

"I couldn't!" Lucilla cried out, thinking of her old home – sad and empty, no lights shining in the windows, no happy voices echoing through the lovely rooms.

"I could not bear to see it again!"

"Don't you think that your Mama would want you to have her lovely clothes?" Nanny asked.

'Of course,' Lucilla thought, 'Mama would hate the idea of her best dresses and coats and hats being sold to strangers.'

Nanny was still talking and her voice had taken on the determined tone that Lucilla recalled all too well from her childhood.

"Now that I have had some time to think about it," the old lady was saying now, "I have decided that I really would very much like to go to Paris after all. It is my last chance to see a little of the world and I am determined to do it.

"I cannot go unless you come along too, Lucilla, to look after me. You must go back to the old house and find something to wear. I will book the Stationmaster's pony and trap and you can go there tomorrow. It's not far at all to Wellsprings Place."

And Lucilla knew that indeed Nanny had made up her mind, as when she spoke in that tone of voice, she could not be argued with.

*

Just after noon on the following day, the pony and trap, driven by the Stationmaster's young nephew, drew up in front of the wide curved steps that led up to the front door of Wellsprings Place.

As Lucilla stepped down from the trap and climbed the steps, her anxious thoughts of Paris, the Marquis and Ethel all melted away and she found herself lost in all her precious memories of the past.

How many times through her childhood and young womanhood she had run up to the front door, knowing that a warm and loving welcome awaited her.

As soon as she was inside the house, her Mama would call her into the parlour to sit by the blazing fire and tell her all about her walk, her ride or her visit to a friend's house.

And then, a little later, her Papa would come out from his study to join them, bringing a book he thought Lucilla might like to read.

She reached up to tug on the handle of the metal bell-pull and heard the bell jangling deep inside the house, but no one came.

Lucilla rang again and felt her chest grow tight, as she waited and still no one answered. Maybe the servants had been sent away and the house was completely empty.

She could not go back now that she had come all this way.

"Wait for me!" she called out to the Stationmaster's nephew, who was standing by the pony's head. "I will try and get in another way."

As she walked around to the back of the house, she noticed that little blades of grass were growing up through the flagstones of the terrace. By summer the whole place would look like a wilderness.

When she reached the tall windows of the library, that looked out over the gardens at the back of the house, there was, just as she remembered it, a broken catch on one of them.

It was easy for Lucilla to push the window open and climb in.

The library smelt of the leather bindings of books and of cigar smoke and it shocked her to realise that her Papa was not actually there, sitting in one of the armchairs reading.

She hurried into the hall and up the stairs to her Mama's room, not daring to stop and look at anything, for there was a great weight of sadness inside her and she did not want to let it break through until she had finished what she intended to do.

The air in her Mama's bedroom was very still and smelled so strongly of her gardenia perfume that Lucilla stopped in the doorway breathing it in.

On the dressing table, lit up by the winter sunlight that was shining in through the window, she could see the silver-backed brushes and all the pretty bottles and jars, laid out as if her Mama was still using them every day.

Lucilla stepped into the room and found herself walking over to the dressing table and sitting down on the stool in front of it.

"Mama?" she then whispered, for suddenly she felt a flash of happiness pass through her, as it used to when she was a child as she came and ran into her mother's arms for a hug.

"Mama – " she said. "I – might go to Paris – "

The feeling of happiness suddenly increased and it was just as if her mother was standing beside her, laughing and smiling and reaching out to give her a kiss.

"I don't know what to do, Mama," she then found herself saying, "should I go? I am so confused, because the Marquis has asked me to go and I want to be with him, but – he loves someone else."

And then it was as if she heard her Mama's voice, saying,

"Be happy, my Lucilla! Go to Paris. It is the most beautiful City in the world. Be happy, as that is the key that will unlock the Marquis's heart."

Lucilla gasped as the words echoed inside her head.

Her Mama's pretty smiling face swam in front of her eyes, as she remembered how cheerful and gay she had always been and how everyone around her seemed to pick up her mood and be happy too.

"I will try, Mama!" she breathed. "I will try."

Then Lucilla caught a glimpse of her own pale face and shining hair in the dressing table mirror.

'I look so sad,' she thought and she got up quickly and went over to the great mahogany wardrobe.

Before she started lifting the dresses and coats from their hangers, Lucilla noticed a large trunk, stuck all over with colourful labels from France and Switzerland lying in the bottom of the wardrobe.

Her heart skipped a beat as she realised that the trunk must have been sent home from Switzerland after her Mama had died.

Something made her reach out and lift up the lid and inside she saw layer upon layer of muslin and tissue-wrapped packages.

On top of the packages was a little red notebook, filled with her Mama's elegant handwriting.

It was the diary she had kept on her last holiday.

As Lucilla picked it up, the book fell open and she read,

"Oh, Paris, Paris! I am so glad to be here again. And these glorious new fashions that are inspired by the Russian Ballet! The styles and the brilliant colours will suit Lucilla's figure and complexion perfectly. I shall buy as many dresses as I can for my lovely daughter."

All these carefully stored packages had been meant for her!

Lucilla lifted them out and began to unwrap them, sighing with delight at the vivid pinks and reds and blues, and the glittering embroidery that covered the dresses.

She held them up against herself and looked in her Mama's long mirror, seeing again the dark-haired Russian Princess she had imagined herself to be when she wore the pink coat.

And the new very fashionable, slim-cut silhouettes of the dresses suited her slim figure perfectly.

"I shall go to Paris!" she cried. "And – come what may, I will be happy! Thank you, thank you, Mama!"

CHAPTER EIGHT

"Will *mademoiselle* require me to dress her hair this evening?" Mariette, the young French maid who was maiding Lucilla during her stay at the *Hotel de la Reine*, asked, as she stood politely by the gilded dressing table, an ivory comb in her hand.

"Oh, yes please, Mariette, I have to look my very best this evening and I am sure you know the latest styles."

"D'accord, mademoiselle, it will be my pleasure!" Mariette said and with a few deft touches of the comb, she scooped Lucilla's hair up into a glorious mass of shining tresses.

"You are so quick," Lucilla sighed, admiring the way that the new elegant hairstyle made her neck look very long and showed off her heart-shaped face to perfection.

Mariette smiled, her round pink face glowing with pleasure under her white linen cap.

"It is easy, *mademoiselle*, to work with such lovely hair. But come, you must see yourself in the *mirroir*."

She led Lucilla across the thick carpet to the big gold-framed mirror hanging on the wall.

Lucilla caught her breath as she saw her reflection.

She was wearing the prettiest of all the dresses that had come from her Mama's trunk – a bright peacock blue gown embroidered with golden birds and exotic leaves.

It was her favourite colour and it made her eyes look vividly blue and her hair shimmer.

"Thank you, my darling Mama," she whispered, under her breath, stroking the shimmering silk.

Just for a moment she put the important function she was about to attend out of her mind.

She smiled as she recalled the look of horror on the Stationmaster's nephew's face, when he saw not only the large trunk full of her special presents, but also the many other boxes she had filled with her Mama's clothes.

Somehow they managed to load everything into the trap and then they had to balance precariously on top, as the strong little pony bravely trotted back to Ferndean.

And now Lucilla had everything a girl might need for a stay in the most fashionable City in Europe.

Coats, dresses, shoes, scarves, stockings – all in the best possible taste and even her Mama's clothes were a perfect fit, as they had been almost exactly the same size.

It was hard to remember, sometimes, that 'Letitia' who she was now pretending to be, was supposed to be a stay-at-home and rather shy and retiring.

But tonight of all nights, there was no need for her to restrain herself.

Finest of all the clothes she had brought with her were the dresses that her Mama had bought especially for her – all the bright colours and the brilliantly embroidered patterns suited her perfectly.

And this blue one was the best of all, which was why she had saved it for tonight.

"I think I am ready, Mariette!" Lucilla said and the maid brought out her Mama's white fur wrap and draped it around her shoulders.

"*Oui, mademoiselle*! Just one *petit chose*."

And she then pinned a jewelled feather in Lucilla's hair, murmuring,

Ah, c'est très jolie!"

It was time to go.

*

The Marquis of Castlebury paced up and down in the crowded lobby of the hotel, stopping every now and then to pull out his gold watch and check the time.

There was still ten minutes before the carriage must leave, but he could not help feeling anxious.

"We just cannot keep them waiting," he mumbled, thinking of the impressive list of politicians, Ambassadors and French aristocrats who were attending the riverboat reception he had arranged for that evening.

Why was it that girls always took such a long time to get ready? Even his beloved sister, Violet, who never bothered very much about clothes and finery, had kept him waiting on many an occasion.

Lucilla was usually pretty punctual, but perhaps the French maid he had engaged for her was fussing about something.

The Marquis took out his watch for the tenth time. There were still eight minutes to go before departure time.

He was feeling especially nervous because it was such a prestigious occasion.

It was his one big chance to make an impression, to fly the flag for the proud heritage of England, the glories of her countryside and the majesty of her country houses.

If only Lucilla was with him now, she would make him forget his anxieties. He could be practising his speech for her and she could advise him and then make him laugh, as she always seemed to do.

He was very glad that it was Lucilla who had come with him and not Violet. His sister would have known exactly how he was feeling and would have tried to show how much she cared, but she would have been so worried for him that she would have ended up making him even more nervous.

There was a sudden hush in the lobby, as the hotel guests stopped chatting and laughing, and the Marquis saw that they were all looking towards the grand staircase.

He turned to follow their gaze and saw a vision of beauty – a tall, brown-haired girl in a glittering, brilliant-blue dress slowly sweeping down the stairs.

He noticed the fur stole and the gleaming feather in her hair and for a moment he thought that she was some visiting Noblewoman, perhaps from some exotic country like Russia.

Then she saw him and smiled, her cheeks flushing faintly pink and he knew that it was Lucilla and for once, as she came up to him, he could not think of what to say.

"Am I late?" she asked anxiously.

The Marquis glanced at his watch.

"No, you are five minutes early!"

"Oh, good! I could not bear to be late, tonight of all nights. Do you think we should leave right away? And you can rehearse your speech for me in the carriage?"

The Marquis found his nervousness disappearing, and he was now beginning to look forward to the evening ahead.

"Absolutely," he agreed. "Let's go. And – *Letitia*, may I say that you are looking truly splendid tonight!"

He held out his arm and Lucilla placed her gloved hand on it, as they swept out of the lobby together to take their carriage down to the banks of the River Seine.

There were so many important people packed onto the riverboat that evening that Lucilla was surprised that it could still float.

Black-coated waiters, carrying huge magnums of champagne wrapped in linen towels, darted amongst all the Ducs and Counts and Ambassadors and Ministers and the salon where the reception was being held resounded with excited voices and peals of laughter.

Lucilla took care only to take the tiniest sips of the champagne from her glass, as she knew that as soon as it was empty, it would be refilled and Nanny Groves had told her to be very careful not to drink too much.

"Champagne goes so quickly to the head, my dear," she had told her, as Lucilla called in to her room to say goodnight to her before she dressed.

"And there will be plenty of it at such an important function. You must keep your wits about you, if you are to be polite and pleasant to all the dignitaries!"

Lucilla smiled as she thought of Nanny, tucked up on a luxurious *chaise longue* with a cashmere shawl around her shoulders.

It was delightful to see how much the old lady was enjoying herself at the elegant *Hotel de la Reine*.

But, in spite of the fact that she had barely touched her champagne, Lucilla was finding it difficult to keep a level head.

The Marquis's speech had been a rousing success and he had finished to a torrent of applause.

He had spoken so well, his dark eyes flashing and his whole being expressing the great passion he felt for his subject, that he had had an electric effect on the whole audience.

And Lucilla could still feel the sharp thrill that had coursed through her body when he had looked straight at her and into her eyes, as he began his speech.

For a moment she had felt as if he was speaking just to her.

'I really must remember that I am Letitia!' she told herself, and tried to keep a modest, quiet expression on her face as an elderly French politician came up to her and complimented her on her dress.

"Surely it was inspired by the visit to us last year of the fantastic *Ballets Russes*!" he remarked, his wide white moustache waggling as he was speaking. "You must have seen them, *mademoiselle*?"

Lucilla was about to tell him all about her Mama, and how she had bought the dress for her daughter after she had seen the dancers and their fabulous costumes, but she stopped herself just in time.

"*Non, monsieur*!" she replied, looking down at her pretty gold-embroidered skirt, "I have never been to Paris before."

The Frenchman threw up his hands in amazement, exclaiming how he could not believe for a moment that anyone quite so exquisite could have spent all her life in the backwaters of the English countryside.

And Lucilla was about to seize the opportunity of telling him that this proved the sentiments of the Marquis's speech about English culture and heritage to be absolutely correct, when she became aware of a disturbance on the other side of the salon.

"Why dontcha just gimme the *bottle*!" she heard a loud American voice shouting.

"*No*!" whispered Lucilla, feeling the warmth and joy of the evening draining away from her, leaving her cold with fear.

It was Harkness Jackson, exceedingly drunk, and trying to wrestle with one of the nimble French waiters, who was hanging on grimly to a magnum of champagne.

"Excuse me, *monsieur*, I have to leave," she told the politician, backing away from him so that she was as far away from Harkness Jackson as possible.

She must leave the salon and find somewhere quiet and dark to hide herself away.

It was no use turning to the Marquis for help, as a crowd of dignitaries were surrounding him, all vying for his attention.

Lucilla had almost reached the door of the salon, when she heard the sound she most dreaded.

A great roar of "*Princess*!"

Harkness Jackson had seen her and was fighting his way through the crowd to reach her.

"Lucilla!" he cried and lurched up to her, reeking of the champagne that had been spilled over his coat during his battle with the waiter.

There was no escape.

She could only stand and face him and try to make him leave her alone.

"My name is Letitia, and I do not believe we have been introduced," Lucilla battled back resolutely, fixing him with what she hoped was a cold blank stare.

Harkness shook his head, as if trying to untangle the words he had just heard.

"Letitia, Lucilla, whatever you like," he muttered and then, as he shouted again, "you are my Princess," he threw himself at her feet, wrapping his arms around her legs.

Everyone standing around them was now backing away, their eyebrows raised in polite surprise.

"What are you doing, sir?"

The Marquis suddenly appeared at Lucilla's side, his eyes flashing and his hands balled into fists.

"Who the hell are you?" Harkness slurred, clinging tightly to Lucilla's knees, so that she could hardly stand.

"I am the Marquis of Castlebury and I would thank you to release my sister at once," the Marquis asserted, his voice sharp as ice.

"She's my sweetheart – my Princess!" Harkness blurted out as he kissed the hem of Lucilla's blue dress.

"I think you are drunk, sir," the Marquis hissed, "but that will not stop me hitting you if you do not desist from your ungentlemanly conduct right away!"

He raised his fists, but just as he was about to fall upon Harkness Jackson, two of the waiters rushed up and seized the American by his arms, pulling him away from Lucilla.

Harkness Jackson snarled with rage and blinked up at the Marquis.

"Cash-thel-burry!" he slurred. "You scoundrel! You'll be real shorry for thish!"

And then the waiters dragged him away.

Lucilla staggered to her feet, feeling suddenly faint and the Marquis turned to her and caught her in his arms.

"My dear sweet girl," he muttered, pressing his lips against her hair. "Are you all right?"

Lucilla could not speak, for the shock of being in his arms, of feeling his tender clasp and the warmth of his body against hers was too great.

But she managed to nod her head.

Then she felt him gather her up as if she was a child and carry her to the door of the salon.

"My sister has had a most terrible fright," she heard him say. "I must attend to her, if you will excuse me."

And then they were outside in the fresh cold air and he put her down, so that she was standing next to him on the deck, under a multitude of stars glimmering in the night sky.

"Lucilla," the Marquis asked after a short moment. "That was the man you told me about the other day, wasn't it? The American who wants to marry you?"

Lucilla nodded.

"What was he doing here?"

"I just don't – know!" she managed to say. "He is a very wealthy man – perhaps he is just the sort of person who would be invited – to these functions."

"I thought for a moment, when I saw him at your feet" the Marquis responded, his voice suddenly deep with emotion, "that you must have been – expecting him!"

"*No!*" Lucilla cried. "I never want to see him again in my life!"

The Marquis took her in his arms again.

"It shocked me to see you like that," he whispered.

Lucilla leant against him, her heart so full of joy she could not move or speak, but could only watch the lighted windows of the elegant buildings on the riverbank drifting past.

"How beautiful it is," the Marquis remarked, after a moment. "I am so glad you are here with me."

"I am glad, too, my Lord. I think I have never been so happy in all my life."

"I suppose that I should go back inside," he sighed. "There are so many people I must speak to. Lucilla – what do you want to do? Will you come with me?"

Lucilla shook her head.

She could not face going back into the crowded salon, where people were bound to be curious about what had just happened.

"I will sit out here and look at the beauty of Paris, and think how I shall describe it all to Nanny tomorrow!"

The Marquis laughed and went to fetch her fur stole from the cloakroom.

As he then wrapped its delicious warmth round her shoulders, he bent to whisper in her ear,

"I quite understand that you might not want to go back into the salon now – even though I am sure that awful brute is quite safely out of the way. But I shall miss you, Lucilla. Promise me that you will take luncheon with me tomorrow – just the two of us!"

Lucilla nodded, snuggling into her fur and watched him walk away from her back into the salon.

Then she sat down on a little bench and looked up into the mass of stars glittering in the night sky above.

*

The next day, with Mariette's help, Lucilla chose another of the dresses that her Mama had given her.

This one was made from pink-and-cream striped satin with a large bow at the back of the waist.

"It's just perfect for a day dress, *mademoiselle*," Mariette said, as she brushed Lucilla's hair. "For it is so pretty and yet it is not at all – how do you say – formal?"

There was a rap at the door and Mariette opened it to find one of the young boys who worked at the hotel.

"A gentleman waits in the lobby for my Lady," he said, struggling to speak in English.

Lucilla jumped to her feet.

"That will be the Marquis!"

Mariette brought her a cream velvet coat with silver buttons and helped her into it.

"This was Mama's," Lucilla told her with a sigh, as she slid her arms into the sleeves. "But it feels – a little odd, Mariette. It's quite heavy!"

She could feel the coat weighing on her shoulders, which did surprise her, as it was made of the finest sheer velvet.

"It's beautiful, *mademoiselle*!" Mariette enthused, adjusting the folds of the coat. "Yes, it is a little heavy, but it's the perfect colour to go with your dress and perhaps the dressmaker has sewed a little something extra into the hem, to make it hang just right!"

"Of course, they do that sometimes, don't they?" Lucilla said and she twirled round in front of the mirror, admiring the coat. "And – it's Mama's! I should love to wear it, even if it is twice as heavy."

"Where will you go for your luncheon?" Mariette asked, as she brought Lucilla a pretty cream lace hat that had also belonged to her Mama.

"We are going to *La Pomme d'Or* – the Golden Apple!" Lucilla replied, wishing she could be there now, instead of standing patiently while Mariette pinned the hat on top of her hair.

And then she was free and rushing down the broad staircase into the lobby.

She was half-expecting the Marquis to be waiting for her at the bottom of the stairs, but he was not there.

Lucilla looked around, thinking that perhaps he was sitting on one of the white-and-gold striped sofas.

In front of the reception desk, talking to the clerk, she could see a large man in a grey suit, that, although new and smart, was a little too small for him.

His wide feet were clad in impeccable white spats, and, as he turned away from the desk, the huge bunch of yellow roses he was carrying obscured his face, so that for a moment she did not realise who it was.

Then he came towards her, holding out the roses, and her heart gave a giant leap of fear.

It was Harkness Jackson again.

"Lady Lucilla," he began, a wide grin on his round face as he pushed the roses into her hands, "I have come to apologise."

"Please, go away!" Lucilla cried, pushing him and the flowers fell to the marble floor.

The clerk left his post at the desk and came over to them.

"*Mademoiselle Letitia* – is everything all right?" he asked.

Harkness laughed and then slapped the clerk on the shoulder.

"A lovers' tiff! My fiancée is just being a little hysterical. She hasn't seen me for a while."

The clerk looked confused, but Harkness pressed a bunch of dollars into his hand.

"Leave this to me," he murmured. "I know how to handle a lady!"

Then he bent close to Lucilla and she could smell the sour odour of the wine and champagne he had drunk the night before.

"Your little charade ain't foolin' me, Princess," he said. "I don't know what you're up to with that lah-di-dah Marquis of Castlebury, but I know exactly who you are. And you're comin' back to England with me, right away!"

"I am not!"

Lucilla shook her head, backing away from him.

118

"I think you are! You're goin' to marry little old me, Princess, so you'd better get used to the idea."

Lucilla looked desperately round the lobby, but she could not see the Marquis anywhere.

She bent and grabbed the bunch of roses and then thrust them into Harkness's face, taking him completely unawares.

Then she picked up her skirts and ran as fast as she could out of the wide glass doors of the hotel and down into the avenue outside.

A motor car was parked at the kerb with its engine running and its black leather roof pulled up over the seats, and, as she approached the vehicle, a man in a chauffeur's livery opened the door and beckoned to her.

"*Votre automobile, mademoiselle!*" he greeted her with a polite bow.

Lucilla sighed with relief.

Of course! The Marquis must have ordered a car to take them to luncheon.

She ran up to the motor car and climbed inside, but the man sitting on the back seat and who reached to take hold of her hand was not the Marquis.

He was a rough-looking black-bearded man she had never seen before and his grasp on her wrist was painful.

"*On y va!*" he shouted and the chauffeur climbed into the front seat and took the wheel.

The motor car pulled away from the curb, lurching violently to the side, as the door was opened and Harkness Jackson flung his heavy body inside, crashing down on the leather seat next to Lucilla.

"Gotcha!" he exulted and she was trapped between his vast bulk on one side and the black-bearded man on the other and there was nothing she could do to free herself.

119

The motor car then rattled forward over the cobbled avenue, scattering horses and carriages in its path.

"So, my Princess, what do have to say for yourself now?" Harkness asked, digging Lucilla in the ribs with his elbow. "I've got one over on the Marquis of Castlebury, that's for sure!"

She kept her eyes on her kid-gloved hands, which lay in her lap, and refused to look at him.

All she could think of was how the Marquis must feel, when he came to the lobby to take her out to luncheon and found her gone.

The traffic was growing thicker and there seemed to be more farm carts and heavy horses blocking the path of the motor car.

Lucilla could smell cabbages and onions, and when she glanced up for a moment, she saw the unmistakable metal and glass roof of the indoor market, *Les Halles*.

Suddenly she realised that with all the bustle of porters loading vegetables onto carts and clearing up the mess after the morning market, there was a slim chance that she might be able to escape.

She groaned and brought her hands up to her head.

The black-bearded man shook her arm roughly, saying something in French.

"Oh – I feel so ill," she groaned. "I think it must be the fumes from the engine – "

She swayed forward, as if she was going to faint.

"Help," she gasped. "Stop the motor car! Quickly or I shall pass out."

Harkness stared at her, his eyes bulging with alarm and shouted to the driver to stop.

"I'll get you somethin' – a glass of wine, that'll do it!" he said and scrambled out of the car, heading for a little café close by on the pavement.

As soon as he was inside the café, Lucilla moaned more loudly still and rolled her eyes upwards in her head.

"Oh, I think I'm going to die!" she cried and called out Harkness's name, begging for him to come back.

She gave out a little sigh and slumped down on the seat, as if she had lost consciousness.

The black-bearded man then let go of her arm and started talking to the driver in an agitated tone.

"Oooh, Harkness – " she whimpered and then half-opened her eyes as she felt the black-bearded man standing up to climb out of the car and fetch the American.

The moment he reached the door of the café, she rolled over, flipped the door handle and jumped down into the road.

The driver shouted after her, but he was too late.

Lucilla ran for her life, dodging between the carts and horses.

Her cream shoes and the hem of her velvet coat were spattered with mud and rotting vegetables, but she did not care.

She ran, pushing her way between the pedestrians and then she turned down a narrow street, following only her instinct, as she had no idea where she was going.

For a moment she thought that she had given her captors the slip, but then she heard running feet echoing behind her and the sound of shouting voices.

Lucilla could run quite fast, but she knew that she would not be able to outpace her pursuers for very long.

At the end of the street stood a little Church and Lucilla made for it, pulling open the green door and diving into the peaceful but gloomy interior.

It was very quiet and smelled strongly of incense and of lilies and there was a large bunch on the altar.

She looked round for somewhere to hide, muttering a little prayer to the blue-robed statue of the Virgin Mary, hanging high on the wall with the Baby Jesus in her arms.

"Please, help me, I beg you!" she whispered.

"Excuse me, *mademoiselle* – but you are English – yes?" a voice said at her elbow and she turned to see a thin man in a Priest's robe standing beside her.

"Yes, I am!"

Someone was now rattling at the Church door and she could hear men's voices shouting.

The Priest looked at her with hooded eyes and then gestured towards a small wooden kiosk at the side of the Church.

"You have come to make your confession, yes?" he asked and he smiled at her. "Do not fear, *mademoiselle*. I have locked the door. Go inside the Confessional and wait there while I speak to these men. You will be quite safe."

Lucilla looked up at the Virgin Mary and breathed a quick 'thank you', as she made her way to her hiding place.

CHAPTER NINE

As Lucilla crouched inside the stuffy darkness of the Confessional, she could hear raised voices arguing in French with the Priest.

It was the two men who had abducted her in the motor car.

The Priest was speaking quietly and so she could not follow everything he said, but she thought that he was telling them to leave, if they could not respect the sanctity of God's Holy Church.

After a few minutes, she heard the men swearing loudly and then the door of the Church clanged shut and she knew that they must have gone.

"*Merci, Monseigneur!*" she exclaimed, stepping out of the Confessional. "You saved me, I am so grateful!"

"*De rien!*" the Priest shrugged his thin shoulders. "I could tell that you were in trouble, as soon as you came into the Church. Then those men came and I realised they were pursuing you."

He then told Lucilla that he had no wish to pry into her private business, but he must ask what she intended to do.

"I should go back to the hotel where I am staying," she said. "But I am so afraid – what if they catch up with me again – ?"

"Wait here for a little while," the Priest suggested. "The Church will be quiet now until the Evening Mass. Sit quietly and rest yourself and perhaps God will show you a way out of your troubles."

Lucilla thanked him and went to sit on one of the carved pews.

Her heart was still hammering from the terror of being chased, but she knew that while she stayed inside the Church she was safe.

After an hour an old lady, the Priest's housekeeper, brought her a cup of coffee and a bread roll and Lucilla began to feel much better.

Soon she noticed that the light outside the stained glass windows was fading.

'I *must* go back,' she thought. 'I must explain to the Marquis what happened and why I could not meet him for luncheon.'

And then she looked again at the gentle face of the Virgin Mary, high up on the wall above her and decided that she would wait a little longer, just until Evening Mass.

*

On the further side of Paris, Ethel Armstrong had also noticed that the afternoon light was now fading into evening, as she stood by the window that led out onto the balcony of the Marquis of Castlebury's suite.

"Well now, Dermot," she remarked, her soft voice giving nothing away of the fury raging in her heart. "It's getting dark. Surely you are not still expecting her to turn up, are you?"

She hated to see the hangdog expression on his handsome face.

It was one thing for him to mope around after *her*, Ethel – the acknowledged belle of London and Paris – but it was so infuriating that he should now have transferred his affections to that most foolish girl, Lucilla.

Since last night, she had spoken to a number of the guests who had attended the reception and she had heard nothing from these gentlemen and their wives but tales of the astonishing loveliness of the Marquis of Castlebury's little sister, Letitia.

How exquisite her complexion was and her glorious chestnut brown hair – and how wonderful was the dress she had worn to the reception, quite the most up-to-date and dazzling outfit that any of the sophisticated Parisians had seen that year.

Ethel prided herself on being the most beautiful and best-dressed young woman everywhere she went and she certainly did not like the idea of Lucilla stealing her crown and especially when she was not co-operating with Ethel's plan that she should marry Harkness.

The Marquis's eyes were dull with misery.

"I don't understand," he murmured. "She seemed such an honest person. So affectionate, so gentle – "

Ethel tossed her head in scorn, flicking her blonde hair, which had been arranged that morning by the most expensive hairdresser in Paris.

"That's how she operates, Dermot," she replied and placed a hand gently on his arm. "Look at how she pulled Harkness into her net! She is completely untrustworthy."

"She told me she did not like him. I cannot believe that she would just get into a car with him, not when she had promised to join me for luncheon – "

Ethel laughed.

"But the clerk at reception saw her doing just that, Dermot! She is probably with Harkness now even as we speak."

The Marquis gave a little shiver and moved away from her.

"And what about all this 'Letitia' business?" Ethel continued. "Surely the fact that she agreed to go along with that deception should tell you exactly what kind of girl she is!"

"It was my idea," the Marquis replied morosely. "I knew Violet would be unhappy if she came with me. So I then asked Lucilla. She did not want to do it at first, but I persuaded her."

"Oh, Dermot, you do come up with some madcap schemes. I miss you, dear boy!"

Ethel moved closer to him again and laid her head on his shoulder.

"I'm so sorry that things didn't work out for us."

As he did not move away from her this time, she slid her arms around his waist.

He was such a handsome creature and it was such a shame that he did not have a more substantial fortune. It would be nice if they could stay good friends, even though she was going to marry Mortimer.

*

The Church was beginning to fill up with people and high above her head, Lucilla could hear a bell ringing, signalling that it was time for Evening Mass to begin.

She moved along her pew to make room and a fair-haired young woman in a dark coat and hat came in to sit beside her.

The woman leant forward and dropped her head in her hands to pray and Lucilla saw her shoulders quivering, as if she were crying.

"Are you all right?" she whispered to her, touching the girl's arm.

The young woman turned round to look at her and Lucilla caught her breath with shock, for it was Mariette, her face red and swollen as if she had been weeping for a long time.

"*Mademoiselle!*" Mariette gasped. "Whatever are you doing here?"

"But – Mariette!" Lucilla replied. "Why aren't you at the hotel? I was just about to return there – I thought you would be waiting for me!"

Mariette shook her head and several more tears slid down her cheeks.

"Oh no, no, *mademoiselle*! I no longer work there. The Marquis has asked me to leave!"

Lucilla felt a sinking sensation in her chest.

"Why, Mariette?" she whispered.

"He thinks that you have eloped with an American! Your secret fiancé! And that I helped you – "

"But Mariette – why?"

"The clerk said that he saw you getting into a car with this man – and then an Englishwoman came to the hotel – a young woman, blonde and *trés chic* and she told him that you are bad and not to be trusted!"

"I must go back at once!" Lucilla cried, jumping up from the pew.

Ethel had come to Paris and had somehow found out that she was pretending to be the Marquis's sister.

"No, no *mademoiselle*!" Mariette caught Lucilla's arm. "The Marquis is so very angry. That woman is still there – and she has told him that you are going to marry this American because you want his money."

Lucilla slowly sat down again.

If Ethel was with the Marquis, he might not listen to anything she said.

And wherever Ethel was, Harkness was sure not to be far away.

"Oh, Mariette! Whatever am I to do?"

Mariette signalled for her to be quiet, as the Priest was standing at the front of the congregation and the Mass was about to begin.

Lucilla sat still and let the Latin words of the Mass wash over her. The quiet strength of the Priest's voice made her feel calm and the thought that the lovely face of the Virgin Mary watching over her was very comforting.

She remembered how her Mama had seemed to speak to her, when she sat in her bedroom at Wellsprings Place, telling her to be happy.

'Whatever happens to me, I will be all right,' she murmured to herself. 'I escaped from Harkness and now I am safe, here in this lovely Church. And I am not alone, as Mariette has found me. All will be well.'

Lucilla closed her eyes, drinking in the peaceful atmosphere around her, but then suddenly the Marquis's face appeared in her mind, his brown eyes full of anger and pain and her heart ached.

'Perhaps I should become a nun,' she told herself. 'For if I cannot be with the Marquis, I do not want the love of any other man.'

Mariette was touching her arm and all around them people were starting to leave as the Mass was now over.

"*Mademoiselle* – is it true that he is your fiancé, this rich American?"

Lucilla shook her head vigorously and explained about Harkness and how he had tried to abduct her.

Mariette gasped.

"So you were not running away with him?"

"No! He tricked me – and now I am running away *from* him!"

Mariette took Lucilla's hand in hers.

"It is not safe for you to be all alone in Paris," she said. "You must come home with me. No one will think to look for you there."

The thought that Harkness might still be hunting for her, now that the sun had set and darkness had fallen over the City, was a frightening one.

"You are so kind, Mariette. I shall be glad to come with you."

The streets that led to Mariette's home were badly lit and the tall houses crowded closely together.

Men lounging in doorways called out to them as they passed, but Mariette took no notice, holding Lucilla's arm tightly and guiding her over the rough cobblestones.

At last they came to a big wooden door, where the brown paint was old and peeling and Mariette pulled out an iron key from her pocket and opened it.

"Welcome to the Studio!" she announced.

Lucilla peered into the high gloomy room lit by just one small candle.

It looked as if it had once been a coach house, but now had been made into a living space with a small iron stove and some chairs arranged round a table.

In the corner Mariette noticed a big folding screen with birds and trees painted on it and now a young man with tousled hair came out from behind the screen, rubbing his eyes.

"Mariette! You are early!" he told her in French.

Then he saw Lucilla and his eyes grew wide with surprise.

"Jean-Luc – this is Lady Lucilla, the Englishwoman I have been working for." Mariette said. "She has come to stay with us."

Jean-Luc's grey eyes grew even wider.

"You are most welcome here," he told Lucilla in English. "But, Mariette, will she be comfortable here?"

Mariette turned to Lucilla.

"My brother, Jean-Luc, is an artist. We have very little money and we will have even less now I have lost my job, but we will do our best to make you feel at home."

"Mariette! Your job!" Jean-Luc cried, looking very distressed and she quickly explained why she had brought Lucilla to the Studio.

Jean-Luc held out his hands to Lucilla.

"I am glad that Mariette has brought you here," he said. "You cannot marry a man you do not love. Stay with us for as long as you need."

*

Next morning, Lucilla woke and, for a moment, she did not know where she was.

The couch she was lying on was hard and, in spite of the blankets she was wrapped in and her heavy velvet coat on top of them, she felt quite cold.

Light was pouring in from the high wide windows above her and, as she sat up and looked round the big room and saw many brushes, pots of paint and canvases that were scattered about everywhere, she realised that she was in an artist's Studio.

And then she remembered that she was staying with Mariette and her brother.

She pulled herself up from the couch and wrapped her coat around her shoulders.

From somewhere outside, she could faintly hear a bird singing and then she found a little door by the sink at the very back of the Studio and let herself out into a small courtyard garden.

High up above her head, in the branches of a tall apple tree, a robin was singing its little heart out, just as the robin sang outside her bedroom window at Aunt Maud's.

"Are you all alone, like me?" she whispered to him, remembering the birds in Violet's aviary at Appleton Hall, each and every one with its loving partner sitting beside it.

The robin cocked its head to one side and sang even more loudly, peering at her with its bright black eyes and Lucilla found herself smiling.

All around the courtyard garden were tubs, buckets and big old tin cans and inside them bulbs and plants were coming up.

Lucilla thought of Appleton Hall and Violet, who might even at this very moment be walking out to admire the daffodils.

Quickly she then blinked away the tears that were threatening to fall, as she heard the door opening.

It was Jean-Luc.

"You are looking very sad, Mademoiselle Lucilla," he said.

He had Mariette's round face with a shock of long fair hair and bright grey eyes that seemed to look right into Lucilla's heart.

"Please – come inside!" he suggested. "The stove is lit and soon there will be coffee. Mariette has gone out for *croissants*."

She nodded and followed him back into the Studio, which was beginning to warm up from the heat of a small stove.

"Did you sleep well?" Jean-Luc asked her, as he poured out the coffee.

"Yes, thank you very much, but I am afraid that I am putting you and your sister to so much inconvenience."

Jean-Luc shrugged.

"Not at all. We have our own little rooms at the side of the Studio, which is where the coachman and his family lived in the old days. You are welcome to sleep on the couch at night. And even in the day, as I cannot afford to hire a model anymore!"

"Oh, I am so sorry! It's my fault that Mariette has lost her job!"

"*Non*! She has told me everything. It was not your fault. Don't blame yourself. But, if you will excuse me, *mademoiselle* – perhaps you would care to sit for me, when you are feeling a little better? You have such fine eyes and such lovely hair – "

Lucilla almost spilled hot coffee onto her dress as he said this and Jean-Luc noticed her shocked expression and laughed.

"Oh, please, don't think I would ask you to pose for me without any clothes! That is not something I would expect of a lady like yourself."

Lucilla was just trying to think what she should say when there was a creak and the door of the Studio opened, as Mariette came in with a bag full of *croissants*.

"Oh, Jean-Luc – you didn't ask her!" she cried, as she saw Lucilla's face.

Jean-Luc was a little shamefaced, as he replied,

"I did, but I have explained that everything would be – quite proper."

Mariette scolded him, as she shook the *croissants* out of the bag and onto a plate.

"Jean-Luc! She's an English *lady*! You cannot ask her to do this!"

Lucilla looked around the Studio.

In the bright morning light, she could see that the chairs and table were old and worn and the little stove was battered and rusty.

'I felt as if I had nothing after Mama and Papa died and I went to live with Aunt Maud,' she thought, 'but these two have so much less than I had then. And yet they are taking care of me. I must do everything I can to return their kindness.'

"I don't mind," she offered. "If it will help your brother, then I am quite happy to be a model for him."

Mariette's face lit up.

"It will help, *mademoiselle*, very much. We have so little money and our only hope to earn some is if Jean-Luc can sell a painting."

Jean-Luc had a broad smile on his face now.

"Thank you, thank you, Lucilla!" he said. "I think our luck has turned, Mariette! You may have lost your job, but everything happens for a good reason – perhaps now I will paint the one picture that will make our fortunes!"

*

The Ambassador leaned forward from the leather chair where he was sitting in the lobby of the *Hotel de la Reine* and clapped the Marquis of Castlebury on the knee.

"Congratulations, young man!" he said. "That was a magnificent speech you gave the other night. A great boost to Anglo-French relations! The Prime Minister will be delighted if all the business contracts that are being discussed at the moment materialise. And I think we can count on a big increase in the number of visitors to our country this year."

The Marquis smiled, but he scarcely heard anything the Ambassador was saying.

Since Lucilla had disappeared – run off with her American fiancé – he seemed to be unable to concentrate on any subject for very long.

It was as if a dagger was digging into his heart, so that every time he moved he felt the pain of it.

How could it be, that, not once, but twice, he had loved a woman who had deserted him for someone who had more money?

And Lucilla had seemed so open, so affectionate.

She had returned his embrace that night on the river so warmly when he had held her close.

It was impossible that she could have not cared for him and yet she was gone.

"And where's that lovely young sister of yours – Letitia?" the Ambassador was now asking.

The Marquis shivered.

Ethel had agreed with him to say not a word about Lucilla pretending to be his younger sister, but he had had to promise her that he and she would be friends again and he did not want that at all.

He would be very glad never to see Ethel again, he thought, but there was not much chance of that. She would not let him go, despite jilting him for Mortimer.

"I am sorry, sir," he said, rising to his feet, "but I must now cut short our meeting. My old Nanny has been travelling with us and she has been quite unwell. I must go and attend to her."

"Of course, of course."

The Ambassador stood as well and shook his hand.

"How charming to have such concern for your staff. And many congratulations again, Dermot, for everything you have achieved."

The Marquis ran up the wide staircase to Nanny's room.

Inside the blinds were drawn and the old lady lay very still in the big hotel bed.

"Nanny!" he asked. "How are you feeling? Do you need anything?"

The French doctor had told him that it was just influenza and that if Nanny rested and took plenty to drink, she should soon recover.

But the Marquis could not help but feel worried, as he listened to the harsh sound of Nanny's breathing.

She was stirring now and turning her head to look at him.

"Where is Lucilla?" she asked, her voice sounding dry and broken.

"She is – fine, Nanny. She is quite all right, you must not worry about her."

He remembered how upset Nanny had been, when he had told her that Lucilla had run away with Harkness Jackson.

She had told him that Lucilla would never do such a thing and the Marquis had found it incredibly painful to tell her how the clerk at reception had seen Lucilla getting into Harkness's motor car.

It was as if the news had made the old lady ill, for only a couple of hours later she had taken to her bed with a fever and a bad headache.

He did not dare to tell her now that Lucilla had just disappeared off the face of the earth and even Harkness and Ethel had no idea where she was.

"She could be anywhere, Dermot. A girl like that. No principles at all. Perhaps she's met someone even richer that Harkness and gone off with him!" Ethel had sneered and then asked him if he would accompany her to the *Opéra* to see the latest performance.

At least on that occasion, he had the excuse that Nanny was ill and he should not leave her.

"Where is she, Dermot?" Nanny was now asking, "I should so much like to see her."

"She's coming to see you," the Marquis told her, biting his lip. "So don't worry, Nanny, she will be here soon!"

Much to his relief, the old lady seemed to believe him, for she turned on her side and fell back to sleep again.

He could not tell her the truth, while she was so still so ill.

He would have to wait until she had recovered her strength before he would be able to explain that Lucilla had gone forever.

*

"You love your garden, don't you?" Lucilla said to Jean-Luc some days later, as they stood outside, sipping coffee in the spring sunshine, which seemed to be growing a little warmer and brighter every day.

"I do!" Jean-Luc replied. "I do so like to see all the things I have planted growing and changing. All I have to do is put them in the soil and then *voilà* – they create their own work of art with colours more beautiful than any on my palette."

Lucilla pushed away the thought that the daffodils at Appleton Hall were probably out by now and stretching away through the Park in a glorious cloud of yellow that she would never see.

"Shall we go back inside?" she suggested.

They were taking a morning break, Lucilla from posing and Jean-Luc from making his endless pencil and charcoal sketches of her face and hair, which he said were helping him to prepare for the large portrait he would soon paint of her.

"Yes, we shall!" Jean-Luc enthused. "I have had an inspiration, Lucilla. I want to paint you as *La Primavera* – the Spirit of Springtime with you garlanded with all the flowers from the garden – "

"It seems a shame to pick them all," Lucilla sighed, looking at the fresh young buds that were just beginning to come out in the tubs and troughs.

Jean-Luc laughed.

"We don't need to do that. They can stay here in the earth where they belong and my painter's imagination will do the rest."

They went back into the Studio and Jean-Luc asked Lucilla to go behind the screen and put on the striped satin dress she had worn on the day that Harkness Jackson had tried to abduct her.

When she emerged from behind the screen, Jean-Luc was now frowning, his grey eyes intense, as if he was gazing, not at Lucilla, but at some other image that only he could see.

"I think – maybe not the stripes – but perhaps the pink colour, as a background, would be good," he breathed.

Lucilla lay down on the couch as he was setting up his easel, muttering to himself all the while.

Then he picked up his brush and began to paint.

"I think this will be the best picture I have ever done," he suddenly trumpeted after a long while.

And he put down his brush and smiled at Lucilla, his grey eyes shining with joy.

CHAPTER TEN

"You cannot sit here all day brooding," Ethel said, flinging open the glass doors that led out onto the balcony of the Marquis's hotel bedroom. "It's springtime in Paris!"

The Marquis gazed out at the blue sky, where white fluffy clouds were flying past, urged on by a warm breeze.

Ethel was frowning impatiently and he noticed how the powder she had dusted her face with was settling in the little creases around her eyes.

He could not help but think of Lucilla, of *her* lovely face with its fresh smooth complexion that never needed paint or powder to give it colour and life.

Then he pushed her out of his mind.

Wherever she was, she was certainly not thinking about him and he *must* forget her.

"I don't like to leave Nanny Groves," he said. "She is still so frail."

Ethel clicked her tongue dismissively.

"She has people to see to her, doesn't she? Come with me, for Goodness sake! I don't want to turn up at the Exhibition all on my own and Mortimer is tied up with his businesses all day."

Reluctantly the Marquis agreed to go with her.

Perhaps it might cheer him up to see the work of some of the best Parisian artists.

It was not far to the Gallery where the Exhibition was held and the Marquis thought he might enjoy the short walk along the sunny boulevard, if Ethel had not insisted on holding onto his arm all the way.

She seemed to relish being seen like this, almost as if she was still engaged to him and not to Mortimer.

And he hated that.

Not because he still felt hurt that she had jilted him, but because he could not help remembering how wonderful it had felt the few times that Lucilla had slipped her arm through his, when they walked together.

"Oh, this is marvellous!" Ethel exclaimed, as they walked through the door of the Gallery.

The Marquis looked round at the paintings on the walls, most of which were striking with oddly shaped and unusually coloured people and animals.

He knew that they were the very latest style, but he could not say that he liked them very much.

It was morning, so there were not very many people in the Gallery – and most of them were clustering round a large picture that hung all by itself on the furthest wall.

The Marquis strolled down to see what they were admiring, expecting another bright purple cow or crimson horse.

But everyone was looking at a simple portrait of a young girl with vivid blue eyes and a mane of bright brown hair.

She was wearing a long flowing dress of a soft blue colour that seemed almost to be part of the beautiful garden she was sitting in, as it was covered with flowers.

Crocuses, hyacinths and endless delicate daffodils were sprinkled over her skirt and in her open hands lay a bouquet of white tulips, their petals ragged and pointed like the feathers of some exotic bird.

"*La Primavera!*" an elderly lady standing beside him piped up, peering at the picture through her monocle.

"Extraordinary! Who is the artist? I have not heard of him – "

The Marquis was feeling a little faint and he took a gulp of air to clear his head, as he had not taken a breath since he had first seen the girl's face.

Her shining eyes seemed to be looking straight at him and she seemed almost to be teasing him with her look of unbounded joy.

'I am free!' she seemed to be saying. 'I have found a world where I can be myself and I am so happy.'

"Well I never did!" Ethel's cold voice sounded in his ear. "If it isn't the spitting image of that little hussy Lucilla Welton!"

The Marquis started and stepped away from her, his skin prickling with revulsion as she tried to slide her hand through his arm once more.

"You know – I think it is actually *her!*" Ethel said, peering at the portrait. "And that absolutely confirms what I have always said about her, Dermot. She's no better than she should be! An artist's model, indeed."

It was painful to hear this.

The Marquis did not like to think of Lucilla posing for some unknown man.

But he could not stop looking at her face and could not help a strange feeling of exultation that filled his heart, when he did so.

"Excuse me!"

Shaking Ethel's hand from his arm, the Marquis beckoned to the stout Gallery owner, who was standing a few feet away.

"I should like to purchase this painting!"

There was a murmur from the crowd admiring the portrait and they looked at the Marquis with interest.

"Dermot!" Ethel hissed. "You can't afford it!"

The Marquis ignored her.

He would find the money somehow.

And, although he would never see Lucilla face-to-face again, at the very least he would be able to hold onto her memory and feel again a little of her liveliness and her joy whenever he looked at the painting.

*

Lucilla was all alone as Mariette had gone to the market.

She was sitting with her back against the old apple tree in the garden, feeling the blissful warm rays of the sun on her face, when she heard the front door of the Studio creaking open.

It was Jean-Luc.

He came running into the garden, waving a piece of paper at Lucilla.

"*C'est incroyable!*" he shouted out. "Our picture is sold! The first one from the whole Exhibition!"

"What? Oh, that is wonderful!" Lucilla exclaimed, pulling herself at once away from the peaceful doze she had been indulging in.

Jean-Luc had been very worried that no one would appreciate his work, as it was so different from the current trend in painting.

His initial inspiration and excitement had turned to doubt and he had become apprehensive, although he had struggled on to finish the portrait.

Lucilla did not know very much about art, but she had always felt that he would be successful and the long hours she had spent sitting for him had passed happily for her.

Jean-Luc was a sensitive and kind person and while she was sitting for him, she had found it natural to tell him of her childhood and what she loved most in the English countryside and the beautiful old house where she grew up.

It was easy to be herself with him and, although she did not feel the excitement and the sense of being truly alive she had experienced with the Marquis, she knew that she had found a true friend in the young artist.

The way that Jean-Luc and his sister had accepted her into their lives and had shared their simple pleasures with her had given her a peace and security she had not known since her parents died.

"Oh, a young Englishman bought it. A Marquis!" Jean-Luc was saying. "The picture will be shipped to his home when the Exhibition is over."

Lucilla's heart jumped.

"Show – me – Jean-Luc!" she stammered, holding her trembling hand out for the piece of paper.

There it was, neatly printed,

Purchased by the Marquis of Castlebury, Appleton Hall, Hampshire.

'I thought he must have left for home, ages ago – ' she breathed to herself.

Jean-Luc was jumping around the Studio, rubbing his hands with delight as he planned how he would spend the large sum of money he had just earned.

"You have helped me make my fortune, Lucilla!" he bubbled. "For this is just the beginning! Now everyone will want to buy a painting of mine. We must begin the next one right away!"

Lucilla smiled at him.

"Don't be silly, Jean-Luc! You must celebrate. Go and buy some champagne, ready for when Mariette comes back. I am going out for a little while."

She could not wait a moment longer.

She must go to the Marquis and tell him the truth of what had happened and how Harkness Jackson had tried to abduct her by force.

Just in case Harkness might still be at the hotel, Lucilla put on one of Mariette's dark blue dresses and then covered her hair with a scarf.

Surely, not even he would notice her, dressed like a servant.

*

"*Non!*" the clerk at the reception desk of the *Hotel de la Reine* shook his head emphatically.

"You may not enter, *mademoiselle.* I must ask you to leave immediately! Our guests must not be disturbed!"

He simply would not listen to her.

She had explained to him that she was Lady Lucilla Welton and that she had been a guest herself at the hotel not so long ago.

But the clerk merely looked at her servant's clothes with great suspicion and repeatedly asked her to leave.

"Ah, there you are!"

The Marquis's voice rang out across the lobby.

She turned to see him hurrying towards her, a warm smile on his face.

But, as he saw her face, the smile faded and his eyes were full of confusion.

"Dermot – " she began, holding her hands out to him, but he did not meet her gaze.

"I am sorry," he said coldly. "I mistook you for the nurse I have been expecting all morning."

And he turned away from her to speak to the clerk.

"Where is the woman?" he demanded. "She was due here several hours ago."

The clerk shrugged and apologised, offering to look into the matter.

"Dermot, it's me, Lucilla!" she called out, striving to keep her voice calm.

"Yes, I can see that," he replied. "I wonder that you have the effrontery to show your face here."

"Please – will you let me explain?"

"There is no need. I wish you well, Lucilla, but I don't want to know where you have been or who you are with. I would prefer never to see you again – "

He looked disapprovingly at Mariette's old blue dress.

He might as well have stuck a knife into Lucilla's heart.

She leant against the reception desk, struggling to understand why he had spoken so cruelly to her.

She should not have come.

She did not belong here in this world any more.

But there was one thing that she *must* do, before she left.

"Dermot – I should like to see Nanny – before I go," she asked.

The Marquis raised his dark brows.

"Really? You do surprise me. Perhaps you are not aware of the dreadful suffering your behaviour has caused to one of the dearest people in my life."

"What do you mean?" Lucilla asked, a chill of fear running over her. "Has something happened to Nanny?"

"She has been very unwell. And I have no doubt that it was your disappearance that brought on her illness."

"So that is why you are expecting a nurse!" Lucilla cried. "I must go to her! *You* may not want to see me – but you cannot keep me away from Nanny Groves!"

The Marquis gave her a cold look.

"Well – since the nurse has not arrived, I suppose you may go to her room for a little while," he conceded.

And Lucilla ran away from him and up the great staircase as if her feet had wings.

*

"Dermot, you are an utter fool!" Ethel said, a week later, her blonde brows meeting in a fierce frown. "Why didn't you just send her away?"

"I just couldn't do it," the Marquis replied. "The dear old lady was so terribly glad to see her. She almost became better by the moment, once Lucilla was there. I am not completely heartless, Ethel. I had to let her stay."

"So you let an *artist's model* look after your old family Nanny?"

"Yes, Ethel. That is exactly what I have done."

The Marquis was feeling distinctly unnerved by the events of the last few days.

He had been so shocked to see Lucilla, clad in an old servant's dress that had clearly seen better days and he could not bear to think of what sort of life she must have been living over the last few weeks.

And yet to see her so kindly and gently tending to the fragile old lady moved him deeply, reminding him of the innocent, honest and affectionate girl he once thought her to be.

He felt awkward now, when he remembered that she had tried to explain herself to him, but he had chosen in a fit of pique not to listen to her.

And now, when he tried to talk to her, she ignored him, saving all her attention and all her love for Nanny.

"Even Harkness Jackson, who was head-over-heels in love with Lucilla, would have nothing to do with her now," Ethel gloated, her red lips drooping in a sneer.

"Then he can never have truly cared for her!" the Marquis found himself almost shouting.

Ethel backed away from him.

"I just despair of you, Dermot, I really do! Thank Goodness Mortimer is taking some time off this week. I must start putting my *trousseau* together."

"Yes, why don't you do that?" the Marquis said. "It is a more appropriate activity for you than forever spending your time clinging to the arm of someone you are no longer engaged to."

"You are a fine one to be lecturing me about my behaviour!" Ethel retorted, her cheeks turning pink under her pale make-up. "Have you forgotten about *Letitia*?"

"No, I haven't," the Marquis retorted, really angry now. "And I don't care who knows about her! That whole business was all my doing and I take full responsibility for it."

He was not going to let Ethel threaten him with disclosing that silly deception any longer. He just wanted her to leave.

Which she was doing, tripping over her narrow hem in her hurry to leave his hotel room.

The Marquis heaved a great sigh of relief.

Somehow he knew that she would not be back.

The little scene that had just taken place had left him feeling ill at ease and he went into the bathroom to wash his hands and face.

'I will go and speak to Lucilla,' he decided, as he looked at his reflection in the mirror and saw how sad and tired his face looked.

'I must hear what she has to say. I owe her that, at the very least.'

*

"Dermot, my dear!" Nanny sighed, smiling at the Marquis as he entered her bedroom.

She was sitting in a striped armchair, looking out of her window at the roofs of Paris, gleaming in the sunlight.

"Nanny! You look wonderful today!" he cried out, noticing with delight that her blue eyes were shining again.

"Yes, Dermot. I think I am completely recovered. It is time I started thinking about packing my things, as I am ready to travel now and poor Violet will be wondering if she will ever see us again!"

"That is good news, Nanny. I was so worried, even a few days ago, that you would not be well enough to make the journey."

"Oh, but my dear Lucilla has worked her special magic on me. It's so remarkable just what a little tender loving care can achieve."

"Where is she?" the Marquis asked, trying to ignore the lump that was rising up in his throat at the thought of seeing Lucilla and speaking to her again.

"She has gone, Dermot."

"Gone? Where?"

He felt as if he had been hit by a thunderbolt.

"She is with her friends, Dermot. The brother and sister who have been looking after her all this time."

"But – I need to see her! She cannot have run off again, just like that – "

Nanny gave him a stern look.

"Perhaps she doesn't wish to see you, Dermot. You have not been very kind to her."

He might be the owner of one of the finest stately homes in England and have paid the bill for the luxurious Parisian hotel where he and Nanny had been staying for several weeks now, but the Marquis of Castlebury felt as if he was six years old again, as he stood on the thick carpet in front of her chair.

Nanny was right.

He had not been kind to Lucilla.

He had not agreed to listen to her side of the story or even been polite to her.

He had not been a *friend* to her.

She had had to turn to strangers in this foreign City for that.

"What shall I do, Nanny?" he asked, just as the six-year-old boy would have done.

"So what do you want to do, Dermot?" the old lady asked him.

The Marquis started, for that was not something he had ever heard Nanny ask him before.

"I want to go to her!" he said, the words tumbling out of his mouth. "I – love her, Nanny! I have missed her so much! But – I don't think she cares for me at all – "

Nanny Groves lowered her eyelids and peered at him through her lashes.

"Go to her, Dermot," she whispered.

*

Lucilla was on her hands and knees, cleaning out the little stove in the Studio.

Mariette had found work with a dressmaker a few streets away and it was Lucilla's responsibility now to look after the Studio's domestic arrangements.

It was a warm day and the back door was open onto the garden.

A few sweet notes of birdsong blew in on the soft breeze and Lucilla looked up to see her friend the robin perched in the apple tree.

She laughed with delight as another robin flew to join it, carrying a worm in its beak.

"So you do have a partner after all!" she sighed. "And probably some babies too, if I am not mistaken."

The front door creaked and Lucilla looked round, expecting to see Jean-Luc, who had gone out to buy some paints.

"Lucilla!"

The Marquis stood still in the doorway, as if he was afraid to step inside.

She stood up, wiping the coal dust off her hands.

She did not speak, but could only look at him and she felt a strange happiness that he had come to find her in this simple kindly place where she was making a new life.

"Come in," she said, when she had found her voice. "I cannot offer you any coffee just now – because, as you can see, the stove is not lit."

"Oh, it doesn't matter at all," the Marquis muttered, catching his foot awkwardly on the doorstep as he came inside.

Lucilla offered the couch for him to sit on, but he shook his head.

"No, no, Lucilla – I must speak to you! I have been – I wanted to – "

It hurt her to see his confusion and she could feel his distress almost as if it was her own.

The Marquis took a deep breath to try and clear his head, as he had already forgotten everything he felt that he should say.

"I have missed you so much, Lucilla!" was all he could manage.

Lucilla's eyes were suddenly stinging with tears.

"I am so sorry," the Marquis was saying now. "I – Lucilla – I can't help it, *I love you*!"

Lucilla found that she was crying and laughing at the same time.

"Don't be sorry for loving me, Dermot. I don't mind at all, I really don't!"

"But I – "

And then he gave up his attempt to explain himself and threw his arms around her, burying his face in her hair.

It was Heaven to be so close to him again, to feel so completely alive as she nestled against the warmth of his body.

"So much has happened," she whispered, looking up at him. "I must explain everything – especially about that American, Harkness Jackson – "

"There is nothing you need to explain," the Marquis said, still hiding his face in her hair. "You are nothing but good, through and through. What could you ever do that is wrong?"

And he held her even tighter.

"You will get coal dust all over you," she pointed out, but he did not reply and just pressed his lips to hers in a long and passionate kiss that made her whole being take flight with joy.

Lucilla suddenly touched the stars and understood the secrets of the Universe.

And then the Marquis drew back and gazed deeply into her eyes.

"You are happy here, Lucilla, aren't you?"

She nodded.

"I want to ask you to marry me, but – I don't want to take you away from a place you love."

Lucilla closed her eyes, drinking in the words she had just heard.

Then she answered him.

"Jean-Luc and Mariette have been good friends to me. But, Dermot, I will only be truly happy if I am with you. Wherever you are, that is where I must be."

The Marquis looked as if he had not understood her.

"So – will you marry me, then?" he breathed.

"Yes!" Lucilla cried and would have kissed him again, except that they both found themselves laughing.

"Oh, Lucilla, Lucilla!" he sighed, as he hugged her tightly to him. "You are the best, the loveliest girl in the whole world. I am not spending a moment away from your side ever again."

And then they kissed and time stood still for them both, as the robin sang in the tree and the sun shone down on them from the high windows of the Studio.

*

"Will you be glad to see Paris again?" Lucilla asked Mariette, who was folding the silken flounces of her white wedding dress in tissue paper.

"Yes, *madame*, I shall," the French girl replied with a smile. "Although, I do love it, here in England."

"It is the first time you have called me *madame*!" Lucilla exclaimed. "It sounds odd!"

"Oh, you will soon get used to it. You have only been married for one half day!"

The Wedding Reception was drawing to a close and Lucilla was getting ready to leave for her honeymoon.

Mariette was travelling with the new Marchioness of Castlebury and her husband, as she was now Lucilla's personal lady's maid.

Lucilla gazed out of the window at the beautiful gardens of Appleton Hall, where the first June roses were just coming into bloom.

"Mariette, there is Jean-Luc!" she cried.

She recognised his tousled brown head as he bent down to pat a small white dog that was fussing around his feet.

Mariette came to the window too.

"*Oui, madame.* I think he is with your husband's sister."

Sure enough, Violet's dark head was approaching, and Lucilla saw Jean-Luc link his arms with her as they walked slowly through the rose garden.

Lucilla and Mariette exchanged glances.

"I am so glad Jean-Luc is here," Lucilla said, "his paintings of all the great country houses of England will be a huge success, I am sure."

Jean-Luc had been given a large commission by the Government to travel around England and paint portraits of all the famous Stately Homes.

"I think Lady Violet is glad, too," Mariette added. "Will you take your Mama's coat, in case it's cold on the boat?"

She held up the cream velvet coat that Lucilla had worn on the day she first came to the Studio.

"I would love to, Mariette. But look – the hem is coming down."

The maid bent to look at the hem and then stared up at Lucilla.

"*Madame*, I think you should see this!" she called.

There was something hanging from the soft velvet. A golden chain with dark red stones hanging from it.

"Oh, Mariette!" Lucilla could scarcely breathe with the excitement that welled up in her chest. "It is Mama's ruby necklace!"

The two of them then fell onto their knees, swiftly unravelling the rest of the hem and gasping with surprise as, one after another, rings, bracelets and necklaces, all of them studded with diamonds, sapphires and emeralds, fell from the folds of the thick velvet.

*

"My darling, I am so happy for you!" the Marquis sighed, as they stood, wrapped in each other's arms, on the deck of the Cross Channel ferry.

"It is only right that you should have your Mama's jewellery. And how wise of her to hide it like that in the hem of her coat."

Lucilla snuggled against him.

"Dermot – they are only jewels. You are the most precious thing in the world to me and all the diamonds ever mined mean very little set against our amazing love."

"We could sell them," the Marquis said, his words muffled in Lucilla's hair. "And then we could buy back Wellsprings Place!"

Lucilla thought for a moment.

"I love that house, but – it is only a house. I was very happy there, but that was the past. My future is with you, Dermot, and with – our children."

She thought of Nanny, who had told her earlier that day of how much she longed to hold their babies.

"I am far too old to bring them up for you, my dear, but I cannot wait to see them!" she had said, her blue eyes damp with emotion.

The Marquis smiled.

"Let's keep the jewels, then, for our family!" he said. "I think your Mama would approve, don't you!"

And he wondered what Ethel would have thought, if she had known that such riches had come to Lucilla.

But, she would never know. And she might never understand either the true bliss of love and happiness that enfolded Lucilla and Dermot as the ferry steamed over the waves.

"May we never be apart again, not even for one single moment until the very end of time!" the Marquis whispered.

"My darling husband, we are joined by love from now until Eternity and even beyond," sighed Lucilla, as she soared into the sky because he was kissing her passionately again.